THE MOORCHILD

THE MOORCHILD

BY ELOISE McGRAW

A MARGARET K. McELDERRY BOOK

ALADDIN PAPERBACKS

First Aladdin Paperbacks edition April 1998

Aladdin Paperbacks
An imprint of Simon & Schuster Children's Publishing Division
1230 Avenue of the Americas
New York, NY 10020

The Library of Congress has cataloged the hardcover edition as follows:
McGraw, Eloise Jarvis.
The moorchild / Eloise McGraw.—1st ed.
p.   cm.
Summary: Feeling that she is neither fully human nor "Folk,"
a changeling learns her true identity and attempts to find
the human child whose place she had been given.
[1. Fantasy. 2. Fairies—Fiction. 3. Identity—Fiction.] I. Title
PZ7.M47853Mr   1996
[Fic]—dc20   95-34107
ISBN 0-689-82164-6

THE MOORCHILD

To all children
who have ever felt *different*

Changeling: an ugly, stupid or strange child superstitiously believed to have been left by fairies in place of a pretty, charming child.

Random House Dictionary, Unabridged Ed.

The fairies' normal method was to steal an unchristened child, who had not been given proper protection, out of the cradle and to leave a substitute in its place. . . . The true changelings are those fairy creatures who replace the stolen babies.

An Encyclopedia of Fairies
by Katharine Briggs

TABLE OF CONTENTS

PART I

PART I

1

It was Old Bess, the Wise Woman of the village, who first suspected that the baby at her daughter's house was a changeling.

For a time she held her peace. Many babies were ill-favored, she told herself. Many babies cried with what seemed fury against the world—though this little Saaski had not done so as a newborn. It even seemed to Old Bess that the child had not looked quite like this for its first few months, but somehow she could never quite remember. Likely the babe just had a worse-than-usual colic. No doubt her skin, dark as a gypsy tinker's so far, would lighten so as to look more fitting with that fluff of pale hair—or the hair might darken. It was even possible that the strange, shifting color of her eyes would settle down in good time. The parents both had blue eyes—Anwara's sky blue like Old Bess's

3

own, big Yanno the blacksmith's a deeper shade. The child's were cloud gray, or moss green, even a startling lilac— never blue.

They were oddly shaped eyes—set at a slant, wide and shiny, with scarcely a glimpse of white around the iris. Old Bess, strongly reminded of the eyes of squirrels, shook off the thought. Plenty of babies looked like their great-aunts, or their third cousins, or some forebear nobody remembered, she told herself, and kept her lips closed and her face shut to the rest of the village, and her fears to herself.

She was by nature a close-tongued woman, solitary in her ways, who kept her own counsel until it was asked for— sometimes even then. Queerer still, to the minds of the villagers, she chose not to live with her daughter or kin like other widow-women, but all by herself, in the little hut where the old monk died, at the far edge of the scatter of houses where the street dwindled into a path over the moor. A mighty odd one, the others thought her. *Contrarious!* Some even said, behind their hands, *witch*. But she knew all about herbs and how to cure anything from a sore throat to a broken bone. So they put up with her.

Old Bess did not care to set them wondering—and gossiping—about her suspicions of little Saaski. Indeed, she wanted fiercely to be wrong. But she had never before seen a pair of eyes that seldom seemed the same color twice.

Anwara would admit no flaw in her precious infant. Seven years of marriage had brought her and Yanno only stillbirths. Now at last she had a child alive and healthy, like the other village wives, and would no longer feel an outsider or, worst of all, be classed with Helsa, who was

4

barren. Helsa, wife of Alun, the only man in the village to own three cows, was not only childless but past the age of childbearing. Everyone pitied her, but it was hard to like her; her tongue was always wagging about one or another of her neighbors.

Anwara doted on the baby, and until the onset of the child's strange, persistent tantrums, had bloomed with joy. By now the bloom had faded, but still she glared down anyone who gave her Saaski a puzzled look. She comforted and rocked. She patiently bore the screaming, though she grew thin and short-tempered as the weeks passed and little Saaski grew stronger and more active and even harder to control. Yanno was not so patient.

"Can't you keep the babe from squalling, wife? What ails it, screamin' like a boggarflook?"

"She's got the colic, is all! Sit you down and eat your dinner and leave Saaski to them that knows more about it."

"I know that's never colic, not to go on this long. My brother's first one had colic. But it came and went, like. And the babe got over it by and by."

"So will Saaski get over it, won't you little one? Mumma's sweetling, mumma's poppet . . . sh, shh . . ." Bending over the basketlike bed, Anwara narrowly escaped a clout from a flailing small fist. The racket grew louder, if anything.

Yanno watched and shook his head. "She'll be out of that truckle bed soon, and strong as my old ram. Look at her kick, there, will you?"

"Leave off staring at her. It frets her!"

"It's *me* that frets her," Yanno muttered, continuing to stare through narrowed eyes at his raging offspring, who

5

glared straight back at him. Slowly he backed away. The child's screams abated slightly. "You see that?" he shouted. "It's me she can't abide! Her own da'!"

"Oh, sit you down and eat, husband! I tell you it's colic."

"Then dose her with valerian or some such! But shut her up!"

Anwara had tried valerian yesterday. Near to tears, she made a tea of St. John's wort, only to have it knocked out of the spoon and into her face while Saaski shrieked and kicked with redoubled fury. At her wits' end, Anwara tried a spoonful of honey, though it was said to be bad for little ones. At once silence settled like balm over the little house, and after a few minutes Saaski slept.

Anwara, weak-kneed with relief, snatched up her shawl and ran up the single grassy street in the bright spring afternoon to tell Old Bess she had found the cure. Yanno sat down at last to his porridge, but he kept an uneasy eye on the truckle bed. It was plain they must never run short of honey. Best watch for another wild bee swarm, he told himself, and braid another straw skep to bring it home to. Plenty of room for three hives, out beyond the garden.

Old Bess listened to Anwara's tale of triumph, noting with sinking heart the baby's telltale rejection of St. John's wort and love of sweets. But she spoke only to encourage her daughter. "No, no, my love, a spoonful of honey will not harm Saaski; no doubt it soothes her throat. Many little ones like honey." She did not add that very few turned scarlet with fury (or terror?) when their fathers came near them.

Instead, she slid a few sidewise questions here and there

into Anwara's overexcited chatter, and got the answers she dreaded. Yes, Yanno had been standing quite close to the baby; yes, wearing his belt with the iron buckle—"like every other day, Mother, what a question." And yes, the saltbox was full; the salter had come through only yesterday. Was she needing a handful?

When Anwara had gone her way—heading for the village well, where she could be sure of finding a few neighbors to share her good news—Old Bess sat a long, grim time in thought.

The baby's birth had been normal—she had overseen it herself. And the child had been placid and easy to care for—until around about its christening day. This, as Old Bess had known uneasily at the time, had been too long delayed. Father Bosa, who lived in the town several leagues away across the moor, prevented first by illness then by a late snowstorm, had not visited the village until after the first lambs dropped. Precisely when this "colic" had first appeared, Old Bess could not say. But neither she nor any other witness would forget that christening, with the babe squirming like an eel in the priest's arms and screaming fit to deafen them all. The holy water went every which way, but whether a single drop fell on the baby's head, only God could say.

Old Bess felt sure that by that day the exchange had already been made. In the dark of some midwinter night the human child she had helped to birth had been snatched away to some hidden, heathen, elfish place, and this alien creature who hated iron and salt and holy water had been left at the blacksmith's house instead.

She had no appetite that evening for her soup and coarse flat bread, and what sleep she got was troubled with eerie dreams. At first light she put on her shawl and walked down the crooked street to the little stone house next to the smithy. Yanno had not yet gone to his forge, but was finishing his breakfast ale and chunk of bread. Anwara was bending over the hearth, setting the day's loaves on the stones to bake. She straightened in surprise, said "Well, Mother!" dusted the barley flour off her hands and came to set a stool for Old Bess.

Saaski, across the single room in her truckle bed, seemed fast asleep.

"I must talk with you," said Old Bess heavily. With a sigh she dragged off her shawl, sat down, and told them what she feared and why she feared it.

For a moment they simply gaped at her, stunned and speechless. "You're mad," Anwara whispered in a trembling voice.

Old Bess, unable to watch her daughter's stricken face, or Yanno's still one, found her glance pulled toward the truckle bed. The child had raised itself and was staring straight at her, with wide-open, tilted eyes, pure lavender. Their color changed at once to smoky green. Saaski flung herself back into the bedclothes and began to scream.

Anwara was up in an instant, running to snatch the child into her arms, glaring over its struggling, twisting body at her mother. "There now!" she cried furiously. "Just see what you've done with your wicked lies! Hush, my little one! Sh—shhhh . . ." She patted and soothed and jiggled without the slightest effect, shouting over the racket, half sobbing, that it was lies, all lies, and she would hear no more of it, ever.

"Will you not fetch the honey, wife?" Yanno roared, and himself strode across to the shelf and brought her the jug and the horn spoon. Saaski shrank from him and screamed louder. He backed away, glancing at Old Bess, who shrugged.

"It is not you, Yanno. It is the iron you have about you."

"God's mercy, woman! I am the smith! I will always have iron about me!"

"Then she will always shrink from you."

Yanno dropped onto his stool again, his gaze on his daughter, whom the honey had quieted. "I cannot believe it," he muttered. "I must not. I will not."

"No, nor will any folk in their senses!" snapped Anwara. She held the baby close, turned a defiant shoulder to her mother. "I beg you will not spread this gossip in the village! Think of Guin, ever wanting to belittle Yanno, and Helsa, and that sour wife of Guthwic the potter—ah, what she would give to put me down! And besides, the talk, the talk—and they would all come here, prying, and peering in the window—"

"Daughter, I am no gossip," said Old Bess. "Or liar, either."

Anwara fell silent, but her face was hard and closed.

"Do you not want your true child back?" Old Bess pleaded. "If you would believe me—"

"I *have* my child! She is here in my arms!"

"Nay, wife, peace, peace—" Yanno waved her quiet with a big hand, and turned to Old Bess. "Supposing we did believe you—nay, Anwara, let me have my word now. Supposing it was all so. What should we do then, eh, old woman? How could we rid ourselves of the pixie, or elf-thing, or moorchild or whatever 'tis, and get our own babe back?"

Old Bess had dreaded the question. "There are ways, I'm told." She chose the mildest. "The changeling will be gone in a blink, so they say, if it is only made to tell its age. For it may be no babe at all, but older than old."

"Then we must wait for the great news till Saaski's old enough to talk," retorted Anwara with a scornful laugh.

Yanno thought about this and raised his bushy eyebrows at Old Bess. "Aye, so far the little one speaks no word even a heathen could understand. Tell us another cure."

Old Bess took a deep breath. "I have heard—but I cannot swear it—that the Folk will come and take their creature back if—if it be thrown into a well—or onto the fire—or sorely beaten."

"Fire? Beaten?" Anwara gasped. She backed away, clutching the now silent child tighter than ever. "I, do such to the babe I bore? Whatever are you saying?"

"But that is not the babe you bore!" cried her mother. "That is not even a human child—"

Yanno's deep rumble broke in. "Enough! Let be." His gaze on Old Bess had turned somber. "You mean well, old woman. But I'll hear no more of these cures. I doubt I could so ill-treat any creature. Not when it looks so like a child."

Old Bess looked at their faces, rose, put on her shawl, and went back to her own hearth, her feet heavy and slow with her failure. She had spoken too soon, or not soon enough—

she had troubled her son-in-law, set her daughter's face against her, and only hardened their defense of the baby Saaski. Now there was nothing to do but wait for time and trouble to change their minds.

While Anwara, torn between fear and fury, went brooding about her daily tasks, Saaski lay in the truckle bed uncharacteristically silent. She, too, was brooding. And she was thinking hard.

2

She was not much in the habit of thinking, only of howling her bitter, lonely anger at her exile from all she knew and understood—her homeland, the Folk and their paths crisscrossing the moor, her numberless kin.

She neither tried nor wished to understand the alien human life around her. Through the long days, caged in the hateful truckle bed, bored and homesick, she had done little but rage and grieve. She cared nothing for her jailers—not the young woman who fed her the tasteless gruel and half smothered her with embraces, not the old woman who was her enemy, not the man with his fearful, threatening iron. They might live out their clumsy human lives or die tomorrow, for all of her. They might have their own babe back with her goodwill. Indeed, nothing would have pleased her more than to be gone in a blink, as the old woman said, back home to the Mound and the Moorfolk, leaving this truckle bed to its silly rightful owner.

But she had no fancy at all for these "cures." To be beaten by that great hulking man with his fists like mallets and his smell of iron was a terrifying thought. As for being thrown onto the fire—! Yanno's scruples would vanish the moment he stopped thinking of her as a child—and soon or late, with that old woman's help, he would stop. Besides, suffering his blows would serve no purpose. The Folk might whisk her away from him, but they would only cast her out a second time, changed for some different human child. And to be put twice to the trouble would annoy them. Next time they might drop her into a far worse place, to pay her out.

As for telling her age, nobody could trick her into that, for she did not know it herself—only that she was still a youngling, just old enough for the others to discover that she could not hide.

She'd left the Nursery some time before, and moved into Schooling House with the rest of the half-grown young ones of the band, to learn the work and the paths. Every twilight she joined one of the ever-shifting groups of younglings led by old Flugenlul or Nottoslom or some other mentor, raced with them out of the earthen doorway of Schooling House, across the vast, twinkling cavern known as the Gathering and up the long, twisting, twining staircase of the Mound, chattering and pushing. Silent a moment at the top, then out through the main portal behind the great boulder, and onto the moor—evening after evening, the unruly troop of them, to spread out,

13

running and skipping, under the enormous sky. The open air, the sharp, fresh scents of bracken and heather and stone and always rain—whether past or present or on its way—seemed new each night, too exciting to allow for any settling down until they'd run the kinks out of their legs.

But then old Flugenlul would summon them from wherever they'd scattered, and make them stay on the Folk paths while they did their evening's work. Sometimes he led them down into the wood at the moor's edge to gather twigs for firewood, or along the fringes of the lake below that to cut reeds for bundling into torches. Mostly they stayed on the high moor, collecting thistle-silk for the spinners back in the Mound, and tufts of wool left here and there by the humans' browsing sheep. They found old twists of cobweb for the weavers and cord makers, wild fruits and herbs and mushrooms for the cooks, bracken and leaves and grasses to renew and sweeten the beds. Occasionally a couple of the bravest, Zmr or Tinkwa, stole away to the village and into a farmer's stable, to spend a giggling hour tangling his horse's mane or tying the cows' tails together. The braggart Els'nk boasted of venturing into the farmhouse itself, to tickle the sleeping humans with ice-cold hands, but nobody believed him. It was only the elder Folk who dared such pranks.

Some whole evenings the younglings spent watching over the tiny moon-white Folk cows with their red horns and eyes, at midnight driving them back to their hidden byre. Now and then they did no work all night, but stole old Flugenlul's bagpipes and took turns playing them, or tied his beard to his weskit button and snatched his red cap and danced just out of reach when he grabbed at them.

Before dawn they filed back through the boulder-hidden portal again and down the long stair—often mounting the handrail and spiraling down, one after the other—and back to Schooling House, ready to sleep awhile and eat something. Later an ever-curious youngling like Saaski— though that was not yet her name, in the Mound it was Moql'nkkn—a curious few like Moql might venture together out into the Gathering, the Mound's central common.

It was a vast, airy cave, the Gathering, a hollow in the rough crystalline rock that twinkled and glinted in the upper dimness as it caught the light in a million pinpoints. The light came from coldfire torches embedded in the rock walls, from scattered cookfires around which couples or groups collected and dispersed as impulse or hunger moved them, and from the greenish glow that was ever present in the Mound. There was constant flitting up and down the twisting stairway as the Moorfolk with their dark, clever faces and floating pale hair went about their erratic pursuits and whatever work was necessary to keep the band prosperous and well fed.

Among them the little knots of younglings could wander, elbows or long fingers touching, big, slanted eyes observing the life of their elders—a life freer and wilder but as haphazard as their own.

"I see your mama!" they teased each other. "There! See? That ugly one over there!"

It was a silly joke; only the youngest, fresh from the Nursery, ever stared about, saying, "Where? Where?" Moql was one who at first had stared eagerly around. But then she saw that all the others were giggling, so after a moment she giggled, too. No youngling knew its mother—only that it must have had one. Each mother cosseted and adored her baby until the Nursery took over, then she forgot it and returned to the Gathering and a different mate and the careless life of the Folk, in which a great deal of everybody's time, whether in the Mound or Outside in the humans' world, was spent in dancing, feasting, mischief, idling, and dreaming. Food gathering was a game of light-fingered skill—stealing eggs from the moorhens' nests, nuts from the squirrels' hoards, lentils and milk from the villagers and their cows. They boasted of their pranks around the cook-fires; one had stripped a farmer's honeycombs, another emptied a fisherman's basket as fast as he filled it, a third had shared a shepherd's lunch. The younglings eaves-dropped on the tales and could hardly wait till they were full-grown and skillful, too.

It was a life without yesterdays or tomorrows—life as it was meant to be, Moql thought then, when she knew no other. And it went on, seamlessly, until she and the other younglings had finished their nighttime learning and began to go abroad by day—to find out about dogs and iron and crosses, and humans who were not safely asleep but awake and wary. They were taught to find the paths in sunlight, to note and heed the runic signs left by the Folk on barns or gates or doorways, and to make the secret runes themselves.

Then one day they were called upon to hide—and everything ended in the wink of an eye for Moql'nkkn.

It was a sudden test and a harsh one. That morning they were not allowed to lurk behind things while an elder pointed out a Man, a Woman, a Shepherd Boy, a Cross Dog and a Silly Dog, and warned them of cats—which could always see the Folk and were to be avoided. Instead they were abruptly turned loose to go where they would, in plain sight of each other and the human world.

"But mind now, if one of Them comes along, *hide*," warned Pittittiskin, who was instructing them that day. "Not while they're gawking straight at you, wait till they blink. Then you can do a shape change, or a color change, or go dimlike, or run up a tree, or just wink out—that's best, if you hold your breath till you can slip behind a rock or something. But don't let Them see, you hear? You'll endanger the Band." He strolled away, turned back casually. "If you muff it and get caught, remember about the gold."

"What if They're on our path, though?" Moql asked him, peering uneasily over her shoulder. She found this much freedom scary.

A chorus of youngling voices piped up. "Pinch 'em!" "Trip 'em!" "Pull their hair!" "Change into an adder!" "A hornet!" "A bear!"

"A *bear?*" echoed somebody, and the belligerence dissolved in laughter.

But Pittittiskin snapped, "The paths are ours! However you do it, keep Them off!" He turned away again, took a flying leap into a chestnut tree and began to tease Jinka, with whom he had paired off lately, and wind the long leaves into her silvery hair.

The younglings, left to their own devices, drifted apart, some joining playmates higher up the moor, others searching for mushrooms at the edge of the woodland. Moql found a few wild berries and wandered from bush to bush, with no heed to where she was straying until she all but fell over a big, brown, gray-faced ewe lying in the shade of a clump of bracken. The ewe stumbled to its feet with a noisy *blaa-aa-aat* and galumphed off. Moql, equally startled, looked around to find the flock scattered about the hillside, and herself in its midst, with every woolly gray face turned her way. The shepherd—not a Boy, either, but a full-grown Man carrying a dangerous-looking crook—was striding across the flank of the hill straight toward her, with his jaw dropped and his eyes half starting from his head.

"Hide! Hide! Hide!" shrilled a voice from somewhere, but it called in the secret tongue, which the Folk understood well enough, but only made humans gawk about trying to spot the unknown bird.

Every youngling Moql could see obeyed. The dozen playing a ring game near the crest had vanished, though quite a number of crows, with a chicken or two oddly mixed in, now pecked in the same spot among the grasses. Out of the corner of her eye Moql glimpsed Tinkwa running like a red-capped lizard up an outcrop, with Zmr, already rock-colored, right behind.

With the shepherd's eye full on her, she herself dared only shrink a bit and go bluish like the shadows under the bracken, fighting off panic as she waited for him to blink.

Suddenly a near-transparent shape—it was Els'nk—darted from behind a berry bush and flung a handful of dirt into the shepherd's staring eyes, and then he had to squint and rub them. Thankfully Moql gulped in her breath to wink out, held it hard, and left the flimsy shelter of the bracken to dash in invisible safety across the open space toward Els'nk's bush.

She had scarcely started when a large hand grasped the back of her hooded jacket and yanked her off her feet to dangle like a puppy held by its scruff. She gasped, realizing the trick must not have worked. Why not? She was sure to be visible now, for the jerk had shaken her held breath loose. In terror she kicked and struggled, trying to change to an eel, to a horned toad, trying to turn a fearsome bright yellow with red spots, trying desperately to hold her breath again, whether the Man was watching or not. But nothing would work while he held her. From all around came the cries of the unknown bird as the Folk shrieked for her to try what she was already trying, warned her needlessly that it was a Man.

Then the shepherd's dog rose among the grasses and began to bark, and the voices ceased amid a sudden clapping of wings. The crows flapped aloft, the few chickens stretched out their necks and ran helter-skelter. Moql could not see whether Els'nk was still behind the berry bush, or Zmr and Tinkwa on the outcrop. She could not see any Folk at all, twist how she would, because her captor had turned her to face him and was holding her, still by a handful of jacket, to look her over.

Fearfully she raised her eyes to meet his astonished gaze.

19

"A pixie, all right enough," he muttered. "Mebbe a Dark Elf. What are you, little one? Can you talk a Christian tongue?"

Moql's lips clamped shut. The dog trotted closer, barking until the man silenced it.

"Can't or won't," said the shepherd. "Be y' full grown? Shouldn't think so. Near the size of my five year old, but skinnier, no more weight to you than a kitten." He turned her this way and that, lifted her higher to study her long, arched feet. "Eh, how my little Davvy 'ud like a peek at you! But you might do 'im a mischief, so you might. There's tales of your kind." He scrutinized her a moment longer, then burst into a gleeful laugh. "So I went and caught one, sure enough! I never held with them stories. Eh, they'll call me a liar, over t'moor in my village." He paused. "Less'n I bring you back with me."

Moql squirmed desperately—she couldn't help it. The man's eyes narrowed. "By gorrikins, I think you do know what I'm sayin'." He peered at her, frowning a little. "Here, now. I mean you no harm, pixie." (Moql squirmed again, this time with annoyance. The Folk did not care to be confused with distant, possibly lowborn cousins.) "Here, we'll strike a bargain. They say your kind has got stores of gold hid all around these hills. Is it so, then?"

Moql went still. *If you muff it and get caught, remember about the gold.* "It is," she said—her voice so shaky and squeaky she could barely hear it herself.

The man said, "Eh?" and held her up to his hairy ear. She gathered her strength and shrilled *"It is!"* straight into it, so that he held her away hastily.

"Right, then! Just show me where, you see? And I'll let you go, I will."

Moql knew what to do next—but the dog, a terrible shaggy creature with bright, intent eyes, was sitting just below her, with a tongue as long as her forearm lolling out between his wicked teeth. "I'm afeard of *him*," she said.

"Ah, never you mind about Trusty, he'll do as he's bid and naught else. Here, off with you, boy, round up your stragglers!" The shepherd waved his crook, and the dog loped away as if the gesture had flung him. "Now—no tricks, little 'un—where's the treasure hid?"

"Let me loose and I'll take you there." It was worth a try.

He only laughed at her. "Think I'm a noddikins? You'd be off afore I could blink! Just tell me straight."

"Well, gold's down in the woods yonder, buried. You find the fifth tree west of the red fox's hole. Then you walk a snake length's south and find old Twilligard's sign on a fallen log—less'n the moss has covered it—then you go where it says, and—"

"Here, hold on! Where's this red fox's hole? How'll I find that?"

Moql shrugged as well as she could for one suspended in midair. "*I* know where 'tis. You'll have to hunt."

"Nay, then. You'll have to show me," the shepherd retorted. He gave her a hitch and shifted his grasp to her middle, tucking her under his arm like a parcel as he strode down toward the woods.

There wasn't any fox's hole, red or otherwise, but Moql pointed to something and he took her word for it, then they struggled along what she told him was a snake's length south, which led him through nettles and brambles straight up to a dense thicket, with not a fallen log in sight. Here he balked—to her relief, since she was sore and breathless from the jolting. He held her up again and glowered at her.

"Think me a muggins, do you? I'll go no farther. You tell me straight now, or I'll give you to me dog!"

"It's just yonder," she said hastily, pointing at random. "'Twixt the roots of that big oak. You'll have to dig."

"*You'll* dig, pixie!" He stalked over to the oak and swung her down among the ancient roots, keeping a fast hold on her jacket.

Gladly she burrowed into the soft mold of earth and last year's leaves, and in a moment twisted toward him, offering a little handful of golden coins with the dirt still clinging to them.

His eyes bulged. Slowly he took them, letting his crook fall. He bit one. "By m'faith they're real!" he whispered. "By jings, and I never believed it."

"Plenty more," Moql told him.

"Here, move aside, pixie, let me there," he said, suddenly brisk. "I can dig faster nor you."

He swept her away and fell to work. She didn't tarry to watch. One jubilant leap and she was among the branches, already leaf color. Next moment she was safe in a high crotch, hugging the mossy trunk and fading to gray green to match it—or trying to. She peered anxiously at her doubled-up legs, her hands. Yes, gray green as moss, as lichen. It was all right, she knew how, the other was some kind of mistake that would never happen again. From here and there

22

in neighboring trees came birdlike giggles, in which she joined with relief and delight, her heart still pounding but her self-esteem swelling like a bubble. She had served that great gorm a turn, she had! Now *she* would have something to boast of!

"Clumsy youngling!" said a caustic voice from a branch above her.

The bubble burst. She looked up into Pittittiskin's disdainful countenance. "I did it right!" she protested.

"The gold trick, aye. Everything else wrong. Slow. Bad. Risky. You never winked out at all."

Before she could argue there came an outraged bellow from the foot of the tree, followed by "*Pixie!* Here, where'd you get to? Ahhh . . . that hoaxing creetur! I mighta known . . . !"

She glanced down through the leaves at the shepherd's head and burly shoulders. The gold would have turned back into leaf mold by now. She no longer relished the joke. Stonily she watched as he turned this way and that, calling her several words she'd never heard before, then stomped off up the hill to his sheep.

"Back to the Mound!" Pittittiskin ordered.

"At midday? But we barely—You mean all of us? But we'll learn, we're only beginners—"

"Nay, just you. The others are beginners. You're a blunderhead." Pittittiskin landed on her branch, seized her hand and leaped, half floating, to the ground, taking her along willynilly.

She wailed and tugged to free her hand. "Let me try again, I'll do better . . ."

23

"Give over, now!" He silenced her with a yank, headed swiftly for the nearest Folk-path. "You maybe can't. There's something amiss with you, youngling, I dunno what. We'll have to see the Prince. I suspicion you're a menace to the Band."

3

They found the Prince on his rock ledge a quarter way up the wall of the Gathering, where he liked to lounge on one elbow among his leafy cushions, head propped on one long-fingered hand, watching the antics and comings and goings of his Folk below. He was old, the Prince, and seldom went out onto the moor anymore, except on May Day, or the Harvest Dancing, or Midsummer's Eve. His hair had grown white under its jaunty red cap, and his beard long. But his tilted eyes were as bright and knowing as ever.

He was already watching as Pittittiskin climbed nimbly up the rough-hewn wall toward him, pulling the reluctant Moql behind, and he spoke first as they reached the ledge.

"So, Pittittiskin? A bit of trouble, have we?" He addressed the elder, but his gaze fastened on Moql, who shrank a little under it, feeling much smaller and more uncertain than usual, with no youngling beside her to touch elbows with, or indeed, anywhere around. She had never come face to face with the Prince before.

"Aye, a bit of trouble—about this size," Pittittiskin answered with a jerk of his head at Moql.

"Big trouble can come in little parcels," the Prince remarked. "What's your name, m'dear?"

"Moql'nkkn," Moql quavered.

"She can't hide," Pittittiskin added baldly.

"Yes I can! It was just—I just—"

"*Ssssst.*" She was silenced by a yank on her arm, which Pittittiskin still held fast. He informed the Prince, in a few blunt sentences, of the morning's events. She'd stumbled over the ewe, caught the shepherd's eye, mucked up a color change, failed to wink out, left shelter and run straight into the man's hands. She'd been caught, asked a lot of questions, luckily been too scared to answer. Finally minded her of the gold trick and managed to pull it off.

He made her sound a blunderhead, indeed. But she could not find any actual lie.

The Prince looked at her thoughtfully and went straight to the heart of the matter. "You can't wink out?"

"Aye, I can! Leastways, I thought I—," Moql faltered. She'd played at it, along with the other younglings, catching her breath, holding it until she had to giggle and let go. Nobody had ever told her she hadn't gone transparent like the others. Nobody had ever told her she *had*. "Maybe I—muddled it," she said in a small voice.

"No way to muddle it," the Prince told her. "You can do it or you can't. Let's see you try."

26

She swallowed. "Right now?"

"Right now."

She gasped in a big breath and held it *hard*, her eyes squeezed shut.

"See that?" remarked Pittittiskin. "And you can tell she's trying."

Moql deflated with a rush, opened her eyes in dismay to find herself being studied by two speculative pairs of eyes.

"What d'you think?" said Pittittiskin—but not to her.

Instead of answering, the Prince said, "Try a shape change, little one."

I'll change to a dragon, then you'll be sorry! thought Moql. She tried, but she knew she had never yet managed a real shape change—only small alterations in her own shape and color. She'd always thought she'd pick it up—grow into it, like. Plainly she was wrong. The Prince was chewing meditatively on the tip of his beard, gazing past her—or through her—into some thought of his own. He wore a red jewel on a chain around his neck. It glowed like a drop of blood against his worn green weskit.

He spoke suddenly to Pittittiskin. "D'you recollect—it was a time ago—somebody coaxed one o' Them into the Mound? Great towerin' fella with hair like a horse's mane."

Pittittiskin gave a curt nod. "I recollect. Not sure who coaxed him in. But I've kept an eye on the little ones comin' out'n the Nursery." He glanced at Moql. "It's no surprise."

"What isn't?" Moql ventured. She was ignored.

"Jinka, was it?" the Prince said.

"Talabar, I think. I'll fetch her." Pittittiskin loosed Moql's arm, made a floating leap down to the floor of the

Gathering, and became one red cap among many. The Prince lounged back on his cushions. It seemed to Moql they had suddenly forgotten all about her. Relieved, she turned to follow Pittittiskin.

"You stay here, m'dear," the Prince said without opening his eyes.

The relief vanished like bog mist. For a moment she gazed mournfully down at the Folk moving about below her, for whom this day was free and untroubled, like any other. Then she dropped onto a low stone and hugged her knees.

"A fisherman he was, I think," the Prince said—to himself or her, she couldn't tell. "Brawny young lad. She coaxed him to follow her, see—the Folk *will* do it, now and again—well, they take a fancy to 'em. But she tired of him afore the baby was born—sent him back Outside. I wager that fisherman's sorry now he ever took up with the Folk."

Moql studied the Prince's beaky profile, his closed eyes, his beard that waggled slightly with every word, puzzling over the tale and why he was telling it. It seemed to have nothing to do with her morning's blundering. "Why is the fisherman sorry now?" she asked.

One bright eye opened to peer at her from under a tangled eyebrow. "Why, that lad'd be five-and-fifty years older, from the minute he stepped Outside again. Likely found a young brother workin' his nets and boat, friends dead and gone."

Moql was not sure what *friends* meant. Or *brother*, either.

"Time runs different in the Mound," the Prince remarked, and closed the eye again.

She knew about that, in a general way, without

understanding quite what it meant to the fisherman. "What happened to the baby that was near to bornin'?" she hazarded.

"Aye! That's the question!" cried the Prince. He sat straight up and jabbed a long finger at her.

However, he offered no answer. Moql gave it up and turned to watch for Pittittiskin, who at that moment scrambled onto the ledge, along with Talabar. Talabar was a beauty—her floating hair more silvery than most, her tilted eyes a purer lavender, the curve of her cheek more gentle. She swept a smiling, surprised glance from Moql to the Prince.

"So, Talabar," the Prince greeted her genially. "Was't you coaxed that fisher lad into the Mound, love? Tall young fella, black hair? Quite a time ago?"

She pondered a moment, a long, graceful finger gently patting her pursed lips. Moql watched anxiously from her low stone seat, wanting her to remember about the fisher lad and explain what he had to do with this blundering morning.

She was rewarded as Talabar's face suddenly cleared. "Oh, aye. The fisherman!" she exclaimed. "His name was Pawel—or maybe Harel. He was lovely—so handsome!"

"Ah," said the Prince. "And he was among us here for quite a space, was he not, m'dear?"

"He was, Prince. Fergil! That was his name, I think. Yes, Fergil. But he kept wanting me to go home with him."

"They always do. I've warned you."

Talabar shrugged her delicate shoulders. "So finally I said,

29

Yes, I will, if you go first. So he left, but of course I stayed here. There was going to be a baby!" She smiled and shrugged again. "It was a long time ago."

"This long," said the Prince, and pointed to Moql. Suddenly everybody was looking at Moql. She stared up at them, going numb all over as she finally caught a glimmering of what this all had to do with her.

Talabar smiled down at her. "Oh, is it you, little duckling? What a dear baby you were! Sweet as honeycomb!" With a light touch on Moql's hair she turned back to the Prince. "That's all you wanted of me?"

"That's all. Run along, m'dear."

Talabar left, glancing back for one more smile and a little wave to Moql, who sat gazing after her like a small stone image, trying to comprehend. *She*, she herself, was that baby. Talabar was her *mother*. She whispered the word, trying it out, with no idea how to react to it. The younglings teased about mothers, but never knew—nor asked—which was whose. What did you do if you found out? Would everything be different? Would anything? Not for Talabar. She had jumped lightly off the ledge and gone back to her life. Not for me, either, then, Moql was just deciding, when the Prince spoke to her.

"So—it's all clear now, little one. That's your trouble," he said genially. "Father's that fisher lad."

Father? Moql's muddled thoughts had gone no further than *mother*. Fathers were never even teased about. They barely existed. "Why is that a trouble?"

"Well! You're misbegotten. Half human, y'see. Danger to the Band, having you around." He smiled at Moql, then turned to Pittittiskin, who was leaning with folded arms against the rock wall behind him. "You know of a chance?"

"Half a dozen," was the answer.

"Take the nearest." The Prince turned back to Moql. "There, you see how simple?"

Moql found herself on her feet without knowing she'd moved. Wordless, she shook her head. She was beginning to understand and trying not to.

"Why, you'll be 'changed, m'dear. We'll just swap you for a human child who'll make a good servant to the Band. Half humans never work out 'mongst the Folk. No, never do."

"But—I'm half *Folk* too!" Moql swallowed hard, trying to swallow the inescapable next thought. "What if—I never work out—'mongst the humans?"

The Prince, musing, seemed not to hear the question. "Aye, you're neither one thing nor yet quite t'other," he agreed. "Pity, but there 'tis."

Moql stared at him and suddenly found her tongue. "I won't go. I don't want to be 'changed! I want to stay *here*. I don't like humans! I won't be one, I don't know how! Please don't make me—"

"Now, now, now," said the Prince, frowning. "It's what we always do."

"Stop makin' a bother," said Pittittiskin, straightening from the wall and ambling toward her.

"But I'm scared! What'll it feel like? Why can't I—"

Pittittiskin already had hold of her arm. "Hssst! It's settled. Come along."

Moql pulled back, throwing a last despairing look at the

31

Prince, who smiled reassuringly at her. "Won't hurt, m'dear. I promise. Won't even know it till—there you are!"

"But *where?*" Moql asked him.

"Nearby. But Outside. In your father's world."

The fisher lad's world. Moql blinked rapidly, her thoughts rushing about. "Will I—will I be fifty-odd years older, then?" she quavered.

They both laughed at her. "No fear, youngling," said the Prince, stretching out full length among his cushions. "You'll be startin' all over. Luck to you." He closed his eyes.

Starting all over? She wanted to ask him what that meant, but he seemed to have gone to sleep. Pittittiskin gave a little tug on her arm and jerked his head toward the shelf's edge. This time she did not resist.

Starting all over—Outside. As they crossed the Gathering she glanced toward the stairway spiraling up toward the moor. "Will I go through the door, then?" she asked Pittittiskin. "When I'm 'changed?'"

"No, no, nothing like that. Quit your fretting."

"But when will it happen?"

"When it can."

"But—"

"Hssst!" he said, with the little yank on her arm that meant he was tired of her plaguing him.

It was too much. She gave a choked little gulp, and hot tears sprang to her eyes, blurred the twinkling cavern and the cookfires and the restless throng of the Folk, spilled over to run down her cheeks—confusing her worse than ever because she had never done such a thing as cry before. But then she had never felt so miserable before.

Pittittiskin eyed her in astonishment. "Eh, crybabying, are you? Now, *that's* a human trick, that is."

"But I can't help it! How'll I—do without—the Folk? The Mound?" Moql could scarcely talk for the great lonesome lump of grief in her throat.

"Ahh—don't fret about *that*. You'll forget all about us. Prince'll see to it."

"Forget the *Mound?* The *Folk?*" Moql stopped crying to stare in disbelief, in dismay. To forget everything and everyone she knew—it seemed worse than all the rest. "Y'mean—soon as I'm 'changed?"

"Dunno just when," Pittittiskin said vaguely. "Soon enough, I dessay. Now step along."

In another moment they arrived at Schooling House and he waved her through the earthen door. "Just eat your porridge and go to bed. Leave the worritin' to the Prince." He gave her a pat, then strode away.

She watched him thread through the crowd, then turned into the vaulted main cavern of the House. She found it unexpectedly full of younglings, collected in little knots of three or four, hands or elbows touching, all looking at her. They had heard, then.

"Help me!" she whispered.

After a moment Zmr said, "Can't." He shrugged, glanced at Els'nk and Tinkwa, who shrugged, too.

Their unblinking, shiny eyes watched her, curious but

unexcited. They were as unconcerned as the Prince himself.

She had a flash of recognition that she *was* different from them—half human. It must be human—this tearing apart that she was feeling, when they felt nothing.

Yet she knew if Zmr or Els'nk or Tinkwa were to be 'changed, she too would likely stare curiously but not really care—so long as she still had the Mound, and the Band.

Half Folk, too. *Neither one thing nor yet quite t'other*.

She turned away, wandered out into the corridor, and stood looking at nothing. Then she walked into the food room. She sat by herself at a long table, ate porridge she never tasted, and went to bed as Pittittiskin had ordered. But inside, she had begun to rage and scream.

She awoke, raging and screaming, in the truckle bed. She was shivering with cold, frightened, confused. She was in a low-ceilinged smoky room full of threatening smells and noises. A door banged open and an icy wind rushed in before the man forced it shut. Through the opening she had glimpsed snow and icicles. It was *winter*, then? But only a blink of the eye ago—so it seemed—it had been late summer.

Time ran different in the Mound.

The man was standing over her, staring down. A wave of terror swept her. He smelled of iron. He wore iron. He seemed fearsomely *made* of iron. She shrieked and frantically waved arms so short and helpless that she realized at last what "starting over" meant. Various faces came and went in her line of vision—a woman, an old woman, the

34

fearsome man. "She can't be hungry." "Stand away, Yanno, I'll take her up, poor little Saaski, there, there . . ."

She was gathered up bodily, swung about until she gasped with dizziness and had to quit screaming to breathe. The woman crooned and called her "Saaski" again. She struggled, yelled, pushed against the woman's constricting arms until she was put down again in the truckle bed. It smelled of straw, not ferns and leaves, and crackled every time she moved. Exhausted, she lay still, hoping to sleep and wake up back in the Mound. Or even to forget, as Pittittiskin had promised. But she woke up still in her prison.

For days that stretched into weeks she dreamed of the Mound but awoke still there in the low-ceilinged little room smelling of wood smoke. The iron man clumped in and out. The woman moved here and there, clattering some things and thumping others. But she herself seldom dared stir from the truckle bed. Once or twice, waking to find herself alone in the house, she fought free of the covers, scampered across the floor on her too-short little legs, and took a run around the room and up the wall just for the joy of movement. A startled face at the window one day put an end to that. She barely made it back under the sheepskin before a sharp-eyed neighbor woman was in the room and staring down at her. When the woman of the house came home and found them so, there was a hideous argle-bargle that made her ears ring.

After that, she could scarcely move but what the woman Anwara was there beside her, smothering her in wrappings as tight as a moth's cocoon, picking her up and putting her down and when she protested, offering her poisons like St. John's wort.

Moql hated the truckle bed and scorned the woman and feared the man and never stopped raging unless she was so tired she had to sleep.

Until the day the old woman came and told them she was a changeling, and the dreadful things they could do about it. That day she realized that there was to be no escape, even in forgetting. Pittittiskin had lied—or the Prince had not seen to it.

Painfully she forced herself to accept it. She'd been a blunderhead again; she saw now that she must try on her own to forget the Mound, instead of screaming to get back there. She must scream only enough to get the honey and ease the endless tedium. She must try to act like a human child. She must playact learning the simpleton speech she already understood well, and pretend she could no more climb a wall than an ordinary baby. She must blot out all she knew—except to beware of that old woman, which she must never forget.

She did not really believe she could do any of these things, but she began trying, and it began to work. To keep herself from thinking of the Folk-paths and the Prince and the cookfires and the twinkling lights of the Gathering, she counted the stones in the cottage wall, the bowls on the shelf, the birch boughs holding up the thatch, and listened closely to the kettle's song or watched the ribbon of smoke as it curled up from the hearth to swirl out the hole in the roof. She pretended she had never seen heather or sat in a treetop; that she had never been anyone but

Saaski. And slowly the door to memory swung shut. The speech around her became mysterious; she began to learn it anew. She waved her tiny arms and legs and as they grew longer and stronger she began to crawl, then stand, then stagger from the cot to Anwara, from Anwara to the cot— and sometimes to Yanno, of whom she was no longer terrified, only wary without quite knowing why.

In this way—doubtless just as the Prince had arranged it—she buried deep within herself the knowledge that she had once been Moql.

4

So the squalling and screaming at the blacksmith's house dwindled to normal levels, to the profound relief of Yanno and Anwara, who gave thanks on their knees for the colic's end.

The neighbors were relieved too, but the gossip among the women around the village well did not end with the colic. Helsa, the wife of Alun, still claimed she had once seen Anwara's infant leap from the truckle bed and run straight up the wall to perch catlike on a rafter.

"A body can be mistaken," said the miller's wife, Berenda.

"I was *not* mistaken. The Devil hisself couldn't make me say else."

The others refrained from comment. Nobody (apart from Old Bess, who had her secret reasons) believed Helsa's story. They thought she'd snooped into Anwara's house one day, and been caught at it. But everybody—except Anwara, who was plainly betwattled—admitted the child was strange.

"So out of the ordinary!" said Berenda. "I'm sure none of mine ever behaved so." She threw a complacent glance down at her own little Pellia—the youngest of eight—who was clinging to her apron, sucking a thumb.

"Aye, you've the good fortune for certain. Your young ones are perfectly ordinary," commented a new voice dryly. Old Bess had appeared beside them unnoticed, as she so often did. "And now it may be we can all talk about something else."

There was a brief silence. Faeran, the potter's wife, tittered. Berenda's color was rather high, but no one cared to annoy Old Bess, so the subject was changed.

Old Bess doubted that the gossip was even well started. But she was glad for Anwara and Yanno's sake that Saaski had quieted, and even began to hope that her ill-timed mention of changelings had been forgiven. Not forgotten. Whenever she entered Anwara's house, the little one fixed an uneasy gaze on her and kept it there as long as she stayed—and Yanno often brooded. However, she said no more, only waited.

A year went by, then others, and Saaski grew from an ill-favored baby into an odd, outlandish-looking little girl.

No one dared say so; Anwara would turn like a tiger on anyone venturing a comment. But all you needed, thought Old Bess, were eyes in your head. The other village children were red cheeked and sturdy, ranging from brunette to blond like ordinary Christians. Saaski's dusky skin had never lightened, while her wild bush of hair was paler than ever. She was wiry and small for her age, her slight little body topped with a head that seemed large because of all that hair framing a pointy-chinned, snub-nosed face. To Old Bess she seemed too strong for her size, with longer fingers and toes than was common. But if Saaski spied anyone frowning at them, those same fingers and toes suddenly looked as short and chubby as any child's—though Old Bess could never quite decide whether any real change had occurred.

It was otherwise with the child's eyes, which were as variable as ever, shifting from green to smoky gray to match her moods, with glimpses of that startling lilac when she was into mischief—and to a mirrorlike dark that was a defense, Old Bess was sure, against the stares.

There were always stares, and more than one villager crossed himself as Saaski ran by, for the tales had never quit circulating. There was the poor yield of Yanno's pea crop one year, and the weevils that got into everybody's barley malt the next—both were whispered to be Saaski's doing. When Guthwic's old cow dropped a two-headed calf, it was soon blamed on *that child* having "overlooked" the animal in its labor. No use pointing out that Guthwic's half-grown boys had been there, looking, too.

Old Bess did her best to stifle the gossip, but day or night Saaski was up to something. She seemed to need little sleep, felt no sensible fear of darkness, and could see as well at midnight as at noon. Despite her frantic parents' warnings, she would slip outdoors in the wee hours, scramble up onto the thatch and watch the moon awhile, or wander into the night. She was forever missing, and Yanno fetching her back from the woods or—oftener—from the moor. Plainly more at home in the wild than in the cottage, thought Old Bess. She held her tongue, but the word she never spoke tolled like a bell in the back of her mind. Sometimes she was tempted to take matters into her own hands and try one of the drastic cures.

Her best chance came late one autumn. The morning Saaski turned six, Yanno decreed that she must begin to do her share of the family labor, and sent her out with the other little ones to gather firewood. It was her first such encounter without Anwara somewhere near. By then all the young of the village had overheard much of their elders' talk. Old Bess, gathering leaves and silverweed in the edge of the woods, heard piping voices and drifted silently closer.

"I know you. You're the smith's Saaski." It was Berenda's little Raab talking.

After a moment: "Aye, the smith's my da'. Who's yours?"

"Guin the miller. We've got a hun'erd sheep. And a horse. My da' owns the mill. I've got four brothers and three sisters. You haven't got any."

No reply.

"I know 'cause my mother told me. Here—Oran! It's the smith's girl. That one."

Other voices: "The freaky-odd one?" "Bretla, cross yourself. Mama said to." "Why, will she hurt us?"

A pause of uncertainty. Nobody had an answer. Somebody asked experimentally, "Are you a changeling?" and Old Bess's heart gave a deep thump.

41

Saaski: "What's that?"

It was plain nobody really knew. "Somethin' eldritch," Raab pronounced at last, adding bossily, "You're not to pick up *our* wood. We got here first."

Saaski: "'Tisn't anybody's wood. I'll pick up what I see."

"Not the best bits. Or I'll tell my da'."

Other voices: "Me, too! I'll tell mine!"

Saaski: "Do it, then. And I'll tell mine."

A thoughtful silence, during which, Old Bess felt sure, a vision of brawny Yanno appeared in every mind. That line of torment was abandoned.

A girl's high piping: "How come your hair's like that?"

Saaski, stonily: "Like what?"

"Like *that*. It's funny. Like a haystack." Some titters, a few shushings. "Your eyes are funny, too. They're strange."

"She's eldritch." "A *strangeling!*" More titters. "Freaky-odd."

Old Bess, now spying unseen from the tangle of hawthorn around their little clearing, saw Saaski standing motionless within the ragged circle half a dozen children had formed around her. They probed, got no answers, fell to squabbling among themselves. Saaski merely watched, her fingers and toes at their chubbiest, her sharp glance moving from one face to another. A bold demand to know if she could truly run straight up a wall was met with apparent deafness. A taunt that the cat must have got her tongue provoked a brief bright-green glare and the tongue thrust out as far as it would go. A chant of "Creepy, daffy, killed the calfy!" brought swift action, not really to Old Bess's surprise. Saaski could move quick as a lizard, and plainly could pinch hard where it hurt worst. The taunts turned to squeals or

42

startled tears; the circle turned into a few subdued small children scattering to their tasks.

Saaski did not stir until the others had wandered farther among the trees in search of twigs and broken branches. Then she faded so suddenly behind a hazel clump that Old Bess nearly missed the movement. Wondering if she would flee home—and what she would tell Yanno if she did—Old Bess followed, only to see her turn away from the village and head across a glade of open woodland used as winter pasture. She made directly for a shallow hollow on the far side, and Old Bess eased through the shielding thickets to the hollow's bottom, where there was a spring-fed pond. *Merely thirsty*, she decided. She found a peephole and peered through.

Saaski was kneeling at the pond's edge, leaning over the water like a winged thing just alighted, long fingers braced on the grassy rim, hair like a strange cloud floating about her head. She had never looked less human, despite her apron and dress. *Now*, said a voice suddenly in Old Bess's mind, *I could do it now and it would all be over*. The pond was deep, one could simply tip the creature in, push her under—in a twinkling she would burst out with a shriek and fly away to her elfland, and Anwara would find her own dear child back in its cot. . . .

Then Old Bess saw that the wide, tilted eyes were staring fixedly into the pond, and realized Saaski was not drinking, had not come to drink. She was trying to see her reflection—a hopeless task in water constantly stirred by the underground springs.

No doubt she had little notion what she looked like.

43

Well, who did? thought Old Bess. The only mirror in the village—a scratched disk of polished bronze—had been stolen by the gypsies years ago. When the light was right, one could see one's silhouette far down on the well's surface, or get a blurry glimpse of color and shape in the bottom of a tin pan—if one owned a pan of tin and kept it polished. Mainly, one looked at other folk and had no real reason to wonder about oneself.

Saaski now had good reason, but that pond with its moving surface would never answer her questions. After a moment she lifted a hand and pressed her hair as if trying to flatten it, sniffled angrily and pulled a crinkly lock around to peer at it cross-eyed. Finally she sat back on her heels and gazed past Old Bess's hiding place, her eyes fading to grayish mauve and her odd little face forlorn. Old Bess found herself curiously shaken, her thoughts in a tangle.

Poor unblessed creature, it may be she has no more wish to be here than we have to have her. . . . Does she yearn, as one of us might, for her heathenish home? Does she even remember a place where she once belonged? Did she never belong, even there?

Saaski stirred, took a long breath. She leaned over the pool once more, and this time drank deep. It would have been even easier now to tip her in before she could save herself, but Old Bess could no longer imagine doing so. In a moment Saaski stood up, brushed vaguely at the mud on her apron, and set off toward the woods and her task. Old Bess watched till the small figure was out of sight among the trees, then took up the bundle of herbs she had gathered, and walked slowly home.

She asked herself often, in the next few years, why she had not acted when she could—if it would not have been kinder to do so. She got no answer. But as she observed the children and Saaski growing up with them, it all seemed oddly familiar. She could have predicted that they would soon cease gaping and accept Saaski's share in their common tasks. She knew they would never count her one of them, or include her in their games. A "strangeling"—that was well said. It was the same as their grandparents had decided, years ago, about Old Bess herself.

Several days after that first wood gathering, Saaski, squatting beside the hearth to turn Anwara's loaves, asked suddenly, "What's a changeling?"

Abrupt silence. It lasted so long that she turned to see if Anwara had left the room. But there she sat, rigid as the churn beside her, clutching the plunger's handle as if her hands had frozen to it.

"Mumma?" said Saaski, half alarmed.

Jerkily, the plunger began again its sloshing and thumping. "Now where did you hear that word?" asked Anwara, in a voice carefully careless.

"Eh—one of the young 'uns . . . said it . . ." Saaski shrugged the rest off. "What is it, then?" she muttered.

"Just an old tale. Nothing to it, like as not." Anwara paused, forced a smile. "Fairies' prank, is what I've heard. The little imp-things put a stick of firewood or some such in a baby's cradle and do a hoaxing charm—and nobody ever knows the difference!" Anwara sniffed contemptuously. "Likely story! Fancy a mumma not knowing her own child!"

"Sounds witless," said Saaski, staring. Whoever'd not know a stick of wood from a live baby, charm or not? If that was all, it was certain-sure *she* was no changeling. Stick of wood! Just more of the young ones' plaguing. Passel of numps, they were.

On the whole, after the first sting of anger and disappointment, she was more relieved than not to be an outcast, and found the children as alien as they found her. She thought their play stupid, their company tiresome. They could do nothing much and never tried, climbed trees like inchworms, scratching their legs and puffing with every hitch. Her own swift scampering caused stares and nudges that made her cautious. Being different made her uneasy, though she had forgotten why. By the time she was nine years old she had schooled herself to move as they moved— when anyone was watching. But it was like living in fetters.

She escaped to the moor whenever she could, despite Anwara's fears and Yanno's stern warnings of its dangers. Sometimes, roaming there alone, or perched on a grassy hillock watching the sheep graze and listening for the curlew's hollow cry, strange pictures stirred in her mind—a wisp of color, an echo of sounds—as if she had once known them in a dream. But the older she grew, the less she was able to bring the dream-pictures clearer, however hard she tried. And she had a wary feeling that she should not try— should not study the faint markings that traced a luminous pattern across the bog and ask herself what they were, but only be careful to stay off them. If now and then she heard the cries of birds she could not name, she hastily shut her ears, the back of her neck prickling, and hurried down to the village and her neglected tasks, preferring Anwara's scolding to the bleak loneliness that crept over her at those sounds.

It was no better in the cottage. She was lonely there, too—in the village, everywhere. She toughened herself to accept that life would always be so.

And then, in the spring she was eleven, the tinker Bruman wandered through the village and up onto the moor in his hooded pony cart, with his three goats, his old dog Warrior, and his orphan boy Tam.

PART II

5

Saaski had already had one encounter that morning, unexpected and unwelcome. Indeed, the whole day had started out poorly. She had neglected to turn the bread on the hearth while Anwara was at the well, and four of the six loaves had burned—one worse than the others. Therefore that one, Yanno decreed when he came in from stirring up the coals in his forge, should be her breakfast.

Anwara hurried to her defense, tried to hustle the burnt loaf into the fire and out of the argument. Yanno retrieved it, lifted Saaski in his big, calloused hands, and set her firmly down in front of it at the table. "'Tis only right. Because she was careless we eat burnt bread. She shall eat the burntest."

Anwara, tight-lipped, immediately broke the best piece off her loaf and slid it over to Saaski.

Saaski pushed it back to her with a shrug. "I was careless," she said, and began to eat the burnt loaf. She saw Anwara's face stiffen and realized with a familiar sinking feeling that she had again said the wrong thing—done the wrong thing. But why? Burnt bread did not seem a matter for emotion. And she had *not* been watching the loaves. She had been outside in the dooryard staring at the splintery wooden wall of the lean-to where Yanno and his brother-in-law Siward kept their cow and its yearling calf. At dusk yestereve she thought she had glimpsed an odd mark on that wall. This morning she had looked again, and there it was—faint and slightly glimmering in the early light, half lost in the roughness of the wood, but there, all the same. She'd stood squinting at it while the loaves behind her in the kitchen burned.

The burntest was her fair portion.

It was also bitter and hard as rock. She hid most of it in her apron to give to the birds, and escaped to her morning duty, which was to milk the cow and drive it to pasture in the Highfield.

The mark was gone from the shed wall when she hurried outside lugging the heavy wooden pail by its rope handle, pulling up her hood against the light rain. Or else she had forgotten where to look. She stood searching the splintery surface until Anwara came to the doorway to shoo one of the hens out, and spoke to her sharply. Then she made haste into the shed.

The calf was loose from its tie and standing spraddle-legged beside its mother, nuzzling her bag.

"Here, then! Stop it, y' great gawk," cried Saaski, dropping the pail and grabbing the calf around the neck, yanking its head aside. She did not think it had been sucking; it had grown so lanky that it could scarcely stoop low enough to reach the teats. But it had slipped its head yoke, which still hung from the iron bar Yanno had fixed to the opposite wall. Leading it there by its ear, Saaski reached for the yoke and stopped in midmotion. The hook was loose from the ring.

"Now, then," Saaski muttered to her captive. "If you're not the first beast I ever saw could undo its own tie."

The calf bawled and tried to shake free. Saaski tugged it into place and gingerly hooked the chains around its neck, shivering a little and scrubbing her hands against her skirt to wipe off the smarting sting of iron. She peered closely at hook and ring; they were sound as ever.

This was her cousins' doing. The cow alone was her task; its calf was the charge of Morgan and Eluna, twin daughters of Yanno's sister Ebba and her husband. Siward and Yanno had fixed the children's duties the moment the calf was born.

So it's Morgan'll be ticked off, not me, thought Saaski, and went over to milk the cow, catching up the one-legged stool on her way. She settled the wooden pail between her knees and her head in the cow's flank as Anwara had taught her, and reached for the teats. At the first touch she knew she was too late. The calf had suckled after all—or the cow had been milked.

But how could that be? The stubborn beast was just holding back. *Trying to cozen me because I'm new at this*, thought Saaski, who had learned to milk only a month before.

"Give over, now, Moll!" she said, and tried again, pulling strongly at the teats.

But old Moll had something to say to that, swinging her horns and aiming a kick at the pail that spilled the cupful Saaski had managed to get. Her bag was limp and empty.

Nothing to do but go tell Anwara what had happened.

So then there was an argle-bargle sure enough, the kind Saaski hated most, with Anwara wanting to make cheese, and no milk to make it, and stalking across to Ebba's house dragging Saaski with her to confront Morgan and Eluna—and Morgan hotly defending herself and Eluna wailing and Ebba saying Saaski had lied, and had likely unhooked the calf herself in the night, just to plague her cousins, as she was always doing.

At that point Anwara squared off for battle and Saaski slipped away back to the cowshed, leaving the others to shout each other down. Loosing Moll's tie, she hurried her past the bawling calf and out of the shed. When they'd finished their brangling, Morgan and Eluna would mind the calf; meanwhile, let it bawl. Saaski prodded Moll into an indignant trot that set her empty bag swinging, up the crooked trail past the last village shed and the old apple orchard, around the fringe of the wood above Moor Water. With the apple trees between her and the village, she allowed the cow to fall back to a walk and go at her own pace up the winding hillside trail to the pasture.

The other village cows were there already. Robin and Jankin, oldest sons of Guin the miller, were just coming back through the gap in the stone wall, preparing to replace the peeled log that barred the animals' way. They dropped it and watched as Moll made much ado of stepping over it before ambling along to join her sisters. Ignoring her audience, Saaski wrestled the log into its socket and walked on across the tilted, daisy-strewn pasture, zigzagging elusively among the grazing animals until the two boys had turned downhill and she was alone.

Over the wall again on the far side of the pasture, she pushed between the thickets that edged the foaming, noisy little brook and jumped into it, shivering with pleasure at the shock of icy water on her bare feet, then waded upstream, beyond the hayfields and the wasteland, past the crumbling remains of the old wall that marked the end of village land, and onto the moor proper.

Here she was at home, and comfortable—and hard to find, as she knew from her other stolen flights. There would be no churning today anyway, and she could gather the cow's bedding on her way home. Perched on a boulder to let the gentle air dry her feet and the draggled hems of her dress and apron, she pulled in a deep breath of heather and broom, gazing out over the rough, wild terrain and the fields and village below. It was still raining in the valley; she could see the curtain of dark gray blurring the crooked line of roofs beyond the woods. Uphill from her rock, where the moor lifted into its high uplands, the sunlight flamed golden in the broom flowers—the only yellow flowers she did not shrink from. Here, between heights and valley, it was something between rain and shine, a pearly May morning. Curling up on her boulder, she blinked drowsily at the sky until her eyes closed.

A deep-voiced exclamation made them fly open. For an

instant she stared into the face of the man gaping down at her, then she was off the boulder and behind it, peering warily at his astonished scowl, his crook made from a trimmed branch, the long-haired, draggled shapes of the sheep scattered behind him—and the dog tethered to his rope belt by a thong. A shepherd. One she had never seen in the village. Yet somewhere she had seen him. And his dog.

"Pixie?" the man said, squinting.

She stared at him blankly, but her heart had begun to pound. He took a step forward; she took one back.

"I'm Saaski, the smith's child," she told him.

"Nay, you're that pixie," he said, edging closer. "You'll not diddle me again, you little varmint. I'm onto you. I . . . I . . ." He stood still, his scowl fading into a puzzled frown. "This time you're bigger."

He's addled, she thought. A real Tom Noddy. "I'm Yanno's child," she repeated. "He's the blacksmith in the village. Ask him yourself!"

"What village?"

"Torskaal! Down there." She pointed.

"Ah, Torskaal. I never go there. I'm from over the moor."

"Well, go there now, if you don't believe me!" Saaski was backing away, shrilling at him. "Ask my da', he'll tell you! Let me be!" She turned and ran as fast as she could go, hoping he wouldn't loose the dog after her. But when she reached a high outcrop and peered back, he was standing where she had left him, scratching under his rabbit-felt cap and gazing after her. The dog had lost interest and was gnawing at its flank.

She dodged behind the outcrop and climbed on until she was out of his sight. She had never ventured this far before, preferring to keep the village where she could see it, whether she went back before nightfall or not. But she meant to give a wide berth to that rattlehead shepherd. Pixie!

Still, he scared her. She kept thinking she'd seen him before.

But no doubt she *had* seen him before, when she was much smaller, as he'd said—in fact too young to remember much about it—when she'd been forever running away up to the moor.

It was nothing at all to be scared of.

6

She was on top of the world now, feeling as tall as a giant with far distance all around. The sun had slipped behind thin clouds, and mist drifted around her, touching her with chill fingers. Tightening her cloak strings, she wandered on, stepping warily now, though she did not know why. The ground was stony and rough, covered with coarse long grass like matted hair between the clumps of broom. The grass was—different—here and there, slightly shining. Glimmering streaks of it swerved around rocks and between the broom, back and forth like the rutted paths the sheep made. But these were not sheep paths.

Squinting hard to keep one in sight—the glimmer kept vanishing and reappearing up ahead—and careful not to step on it, Saaski followed a slim trail into a hollow, then started scrambling up the steep bank on the other side. She was brought up short by a loud "Blaaaat!" so close that she slipped and gave a squeak of fright.

She found herself confronting a large black goat, who had thrust its forequarters over the lip of the hollow to stare down at her enigmatically from its yellow eyes. She stared back. She knew nothing about goats except that they were not like sheep. "Get away, you!" she ventured. It merely began to chew its cud, setting its beard waggling and the little bell around its neck tinkling. It didn't move.

"Well, then, stay there, I'll go around," she muttered, glancing down to be sure not to step on the trail she had been following. It had vanished—or she had lost it. She started up the last steep bit, giving the goat a wide berth, only to see another goat appear against the sky beside it and stare down in its turn. This one was white, and smaller. An instant later a gray one shoved up beside the white.

It was a flock, then. Maybe with a rattlehead goatherd and a dog. She had best turn back.

At that moment the goatherd appeared beside his animals—and it was only a boy not much older than herself, dressed in an odd assortment of rags and tatters. He was dark haired and gangly, with bright blue eyes and a stubby nose. He didn't look rattleheaded. He looked funny, and friendly, and nice.

"Oh, 'twas you, was it?" he said in an interested tone. "I wondered what they was gawking at. Don't be afeard—they won't hurt you. Come on along."

"Nay, I won't go through your flock."

"There's only the three of them. Hey, you! Divil! Git! Get along, all 'a you, go eat somewheres else." He bounced his

59

stick impartially on three bony rumps, and the black goat pushed bossily between the others to lead the way back out of sight. The boy reached his stick down. "Grab hold, I'll give you a pull!"

Saaski grabbed, all but flew up the slope with the vigor of his pull, and stumbled forward until he caught her.

"Sorry! Y'don't weigh much, do you? Here, sit down and puff a bit," he invited.

She had no need to puff, but she dropped down on one of the low boulders scattered about the moor, and he straddled another, tossing aside his stick. They examined each other, he with a curiosity as open and friendly as his face, she without once feeling she must make her hands chubbier and her feet shorter. They exchanged names. His was Tam.

"What are the goats' names?" she asked him. The big black and his attendant nannies were browsing on some thornbushes a little distance away.

"Divil's the black one. The little white is Angel, and the gray's just Sister."

"Are they yours?"

"They're Bruman's. But it's me as looks after 'em. While Warrior looks after Bruman."

"A warrior?"

"Not a real one—just Bruman's old dog."

"Is Bruman your da'?" asked Saaski.

"Nay, me da's dead. Mumma, too. Bruman's the tinker. We pass this way every year or so—camp on the moor awhile—move on. Maybe you saw us come through your village about a se'nnight ago? Old two-wheel cart with a raggedy

hood, pony and Warrior in front, me and the goats behind."
The boy grinned again—at himself, it seemed to Saaski. He
had good white teeth, with a space between a couple of side
ones that lent him a rakish air.

She said, "We need no tinker in Torskaal. My da' does all
the smithing hereabouts."

"I know that; so does Bruman. No matter. He can make
boots, and shoes, and saddles, and harness, and gloves and
dagger sheaths and locks and leathern boxes—"

"But who'd hire such skills?" said Saaski, round eyed. The
only horse in the village was Guin the miller's and it already
had a saddle. The oxen worked under wooden yokes.
Nobody locked anything. And who wore shoes or boots
until snow flew? As for gloves and dagger sheaths and leathern boxes, she'd never heard of such fineries. "I doubt he'll
find work in Torskaal," she warned.

"'Twon't matter to Bruman. He'll find some way to earn a
flagon of muxta or strong cider, then he'll worry about nothing till it's empty and he's full."

"He'll be drunken?" said Saaski, eyes rounder than ever.

"Whenever he can be." Tam shrugged. "Got a lame leg,
Bruman has. It pains 'im bad. He won't talk of it. Mostly just
takes it out on me and the pony," Tam added cheerfully.
"Truth to tell, I'd ruther he stayed drunk."

"But d'you have nothing to eat, when he is?"

"Oh, me and Warrior see to ourselves. The dog's a good
ratter, cotches most of his own meals. In the towns, well, I'm
a fair hand at tinkerin' meself, by now. Had to pick it up,
didn't I, to finish *his* jobs when he's boozin'! On the road I

61

can always find a day's work, and there's the goats' milk and hearth bread. Bruman fills a hoggin with barley flour afore we leave each spring, or I don't budge."

"Where d'you live in wintertime?"

"The King's Town. Away by the big river, in the low country."

Saaaski looked at him with awe, trying to imagine the King's Town, and the big river—thrice as wide as the creek, no doubt—and country even lower than the village. She had never traveled farther than the other side of Moor Water.

Musing back over their talk, she found a puzzle. "How did you know my da's the smith?" she demanded.

"Well, they said you was the . . . the"—Tam floundered a moment, went red under his tan—"the young one at the smith's house. I saw you t'other day, in the village—I was filling my waterbag at the well. They talk about you—the goodwives. Didn't you know it?"

She shrugged but braced herself, knowing well the dropped voices, the nudges, the narrow glances. "Not sure what they say."

Tam kicked at a grass tussock, frowning first at it and then toward the goats, which had browsed their way over the next rise, then answered carelessly. "Eh, not much. Only what they say about any young 'un different from *their* Raabs and Annies. They say you're eldritch. They say you're freaky-odd." He turned back to her, smiling, and she waited. She'd heard that much from the Raabs and Annies themselves. "They say the same of me," he finished blithely.

It was something too bad to tell her.

Eh, what do I care, they can say what they like, she told herself with the familiar mixture of anger and desolation. The chill mists were swirling around them suddenly, the next thing to rain. She pulled up her hood and rose. "I've all my tasks to do yet," she said. "I'll be going."

"But maybe soon be climbing up again?"

"Maybe." She smiled to show she bore him no ill will for a lie meant kindly, and started down the slope, avoiding the steep-sided hollow and the glimmering trail she could no longer see—that might not even be there. He fell in beside her.

"I'm hereabout most days, with the goats. I could play me pipes for you." He produced from his ragged tunic a longish shepherd's pipe made of a reed, and a shorter one whittled from a willow twig. "Or juggle!" He stuffed the pipes away, snatched up a handful of pebbles and set them flying up in front of him, changing their pattern from circle to up-and-down to an arc over his head, while Saaski watched, astonished. Whirling about, he caught the pebbles one-handed behind his back, then strolled toward her with a grin that showed the gap at one side.

"Eh, but that's wizardly!" she exclaimed, the goodwives and their mutterings forgotten. "How can you do it?"

"My da' taught me afore he died. And I've the long day with the goats to do nothing but practice. If you climb up again tomorrow or so, I'll show you more."

"I will."

She looked back once to wave at him where he still stood outlined against the drifting mist, idly tossing the pebbles as he watched her, then she skipped and danced her way down from the high moor to the tilted wastelands where the bracken grew thickest. With the little wooden-handled knife Yanno had made for her she cut a pile of the fern fronds and tied them with bindweed into a bundle. Worrying it up somehow onto a boulder, she backed up to it and hitched it onto her shoulders, slanting it across her back and clinging with both hands to the bindings.

Today, with Tam and his goats and his pebbles to think about, she went through the familiar motions without once losing her temper, and with the frond tips jiggling against her ear went on downhill past the Lowfield where a few village men were weeding the long, greening strips of winter grain, and along the crooked trail around the apple orchard.

Just beyond Edildan's ox stall she came in sight of the village street, with its score or so of stone cottages and sagging sheds scattered higgledy-piggledy along it. Several log ladders leaned against the house walls, for it was the season for pulling the moss off the roofs and repairing thatch. But the men or their sons who should have been on the ladders were instead clustered near the well, their mallets dangling from their hands. With them were a dozen goodwives, white-kerchiefed heads huddled together, forearms tucked under their aprons. A few of the younger children played tag around them, and old man Fiach was hobbling toward them with his dog. Something was up. Their murmuring buzzed like a threatened hive.

Saaski did not see Anwara's sky-blue shawl among them. But she spotted Ebba and remembered with a disheartened rush the cow, the calf, the morning's brangle. Now it would all turn out to be her fault—Ebba would make sure of it.

Then she saw that the center of the group was a stranger, a man with his back toward her. He was telling some tale that held the others spell-struck and gaping.

Saaski glanced regretfully at the smithy and cottage, just a few steps along the rutted street; she could not reasonably get close enough to hear the story—though doubtless she would hear it on every side tomorrow. Hitching up her heavy load, she picked her way down onto the street and across it. She was enjoying the feel of the cool grassy mud under her feet when she realized the buzzing of the voices had ceased. Peering around the fringe of her bracken fronds, she saw the group by the well standing silent, every head turned her way. Even old Fiach's dog was gawking at her.

She halted, her throat closing with alarm. What could it have to do with her? Then she saw the storyteller's face.

It was the shepherd. The Tom Noddy with his "pixie." He'd actually done what she said, and come to ask Yanno himself if he had a child. So had he asked Yanno? Or just gathered the village to set them gaping with his tomfool tale?

Either way, Yanno would know how far she'd strayed today.

Whirling away, she stomped on to the cowshed, yanked open the door, flung her heavy bundle to the earth floor and kicked it hard. She stood a moment flexing her hands, which were sore from clinging to the bindweed. Then she grabbed the wooden rake from where it leaned near the doorway, furiously cleared away Moll's old bedding, and began to spread the new.

7

Yanno appeared in the shed doorway before she had finished spreading the bracken in Moll's stall.

"Leave that," he said. "Come into the room with me."

He turned away at once. Saaski hesitated, then dropped the ferns she was holding and reluctantly followed him out of the lean-to and into the cottage. From the dooryard she darted a glance toward the storytelling group; it was scattering, as if every listener had suddenly remembered a task. Beyond them up the street she glimpsed Anwara's blue shawl.

Yanno lifted the latch, ducked under the low door frame, and stepped down heavily onto the sunken earth floor, shoving aside one of Anwara's hens that was disputing the way with him. Saaski caught the bird and tossed it outside in a flurry of feathers and wild clucking, then followed Yanno and stood warily meeting his eyes.

"Shepherd came to my smithy an hour ago," Yanno said without preamble. "Asked me did I have a child so high." He held out a big hand. "'Twas you he saw this morning?"

Saaski nodded.

Yanno studied her a moment, then made a half-embarrassed gesture. "Said he thought t'was a pixie. One he'd seen afore."

"Said it to me, too," Saaski mumbled. "He's some kind of noddikins, is what I thought."

"He's cousin to Cattila—young Hungus's wife, up the street here. Name's Mikkel. Never heard he was addled." Yanno paused. "Maybe not too bright. You never saw him afore, then?"

Saaski swallowed, tried to say "never," ended by shrugging. "What's that mean?"

"Means I dunno! I might've—when I was little, and kept running off. Can't recollect."

"Ahh, that could be it," said Yanno, and he sounded oddly relieved. Then he frowned again. "Where was it this morning? That he ran onto you?"

"Well, um, up above the Highfield, like."

"That'll be wasteland, but Torskaal land. *Our* grazing. *He* lives other side of the moor. Never comes our way."

"It was on the moor, then," said Saaski unwillingly.

"Aye, there 'tis! Now, I've told you! Stay on village land! You're ever in mischief! I'll lay odds you was plaguing his sheep."

"I wasn't! I was just—I fell asleep."

"*Asleep?* In the middle of the moor there? Child, that's daft."

Well, I was sleepy, Saaski thought. However, she knew better than to say it. Yanno did not like argufying young ones. Instead she chewed her lip and looked elsewhere.

Yanno turned away with an exasperated gesture. "Eh, then, you listen to me! Stay off the moor, you hear? You've got no call to be there. You're never to go there again."

Saaski was staring at him now. "Not ever?" she gasped.

"Leastways till you're a grown maid and know what's what. Moor's a wild sort of place. No playground for snippets like you."

"But Da'—but please—"

"That'll do, now. No argufying." Yanno glanced toward the doorway as Anwara stepped in. "Your mother'll say the same!"

Anwara pulled off her shawl and hung it on its accustomed peg, asking absently, "The same as what?" Without waiting for an answer she added, "What was the great forgathering up around the well just now? A body'd think 'twas a conventicle!"

"Conventicle of gossiping, same as every day," Yanno muttered. His glance at Saaski told her clearly to keep her mouth shut. She was glad to obey.

"Gossiping about what? They broke up fast enough when they saw me coming!" Anwara was eyeing them both suspiciously.

"How should I know? I was at my forge. Cattila's cousin Mikkel was around, blethering some tale!" Yanno waved the subject away. "The child here was on the moor again this morning—right among Mikkel's sheep, she was, 'cause he saw her there. Now, wife, I've told her to stay below the wall—and *off* the moor. From this minute till I say different! You're to tell her the same."

His tone was stern enough to divert Anwara's attention from the well gossipers to Saaski, who stood numb and despairing, thinking of Tam and the juggling and the piping, now never to be hers. There was no use hoping Anwara would defend her this time. She had ever fretted about the moor, scolded when Saaski ran away there, begged and ordered her to stay below the wall. The moor was wild and dangerous. Some said there were wolves. Everyone knew there were treacherous bogs, tales aplenty of grown men wandering off the trails and losing their way, breaking a leg in some mishap and dying helpless of pain and starvation— and other, darker tales of bogles and hobgoblins, of Moorfolks' mischief and the fool's-fire that led you where it willed. . . .

It sounded nothing like Saaski's beloved moor, which for her was wide with freedom and unshadowed by fear. But Yanno meant what he said this time. He and Anwara changed the list of her duties and the shape of her day; before they were finished she was all but house-tethered.

It was all that rattlehead shepherd's doing, Saaski thought bitterly. Yanno was afeard of his tongue, that was the long and short of it.

Her vexations were not over. Ill luck came in threes, everyone said, and the third blow fell a few mornings later. She went out to the shed to milk and again found Moll's

69

bag empty. Someone—or something—had once more got there ahead of her. This time no one could blame the calf, which was now stalled in Siward's ox-shed, across the road.

They would blame Saaski. She knew it well.

She stood a moment, baffled and angry, just outside the shed door, telling herself to go on, go back home and get it over with, but dreading to face Anwara and start the village tongues wagging once again. Suddenly she turned to scan the rough wooden wall beside her, remembering the strange mark she had seen there—or *almost* seen—that other morning this had happened.

And there it was again.

It seemed clearer this time. Fresher. There were three straggling lines crossed by another, all contained within a mark curved like a cupped hand. She stared at it until it wavered and vanished, then put down her empty bucket, found a twig, and tried to scratch the pattern in the dirt.

It was oddly hard to copy. She was on her third attempt when a shadow fell across her hand, and she found Old Bess leaning over her, watching. Quickly she straightened up, scrubbed at her scratchings with a bare foot.

"Nay, child, don't rub them out. Let me see." Old Bess put out a restraining hand, but she did not sound angry. "What is that mark?" she asked.

"I dunno. I saw it—" Saaski's glance went to the shed wall, and Old Bess's followed it. The mark was there again, slightly glimmering, then partly gone. "D'you see?" said Saaski. "It comes and goes like that."

Old Bess gazed silently at the wall, then at Saaski. "I see nothing," she said.

"But—" Saaski went to the wall, stood on tiptoe to put one finger on the mark itself. "Just there."

"Aye, I don't doubt you, child," said Old Bess slowly. "But I can't see it."

For a moment their eyes met—Saaski's puzzled, Old Bess's speculative.

"Draw it again—on the ground there," said the woman.

Saaski tried her best. It was not the same, but close enough. "What is it?" she asked. "I saw it t'other time, too."

"What other time?"

There, now, I've gone and let it out, thought Saaski, bracing herself for a tongue-lashing. She drew a long breath. "T'other time Moll was milked afore I got here."

"I see." Old Bess did not really seem surprised. "So that's happened again today?"

Saaski nodded, and waited, uncertain which was coming—the expected scolding or totally unexpected support.

Old Bess said quietly, "The mark is a rune. I think it is a sign meaning a cow may be milked here—and the thief will go blameless because the blame will fall on someone else."

Saaski could feel her eyes stretching wider and wider. The word *rune* was echoing and re-echoing in her mind, filling all its spaces. It was several moments before she grasped the rest of the remark. "Somebody *wants* me blamed?" she faltered.

"Maybe not that, exactly. Just—there is safety for the thief if you are."

Saaski barely heard the answer. "What is a rune?" she asked urgently.

"A kind of writing."

71

"I think I know some other ones," whispered Saaski, rather frightening herself. "Or once did," she added confusedly. "I daresay 'twas a dream."

"Could you draw one of the others?"

"I could not," Saaski said quickly, unwilling to try or even to ask herself why she was unwilling. She cast about hurriedly for some safe subject.

Old Bess supplied it. "Suppose we wash this mark off the wall. If you guide my hand, I will do the washing."

"Will we tell my mother?" whispered Saaski.

Old Bess smiled briefly. "We will tell Anwara the cow was milked. But I will come with you to tell her. The washing we will do later, when she has gone to the Lowfield to weed her peas."

So it happened. Saaski did not know why it was so much easier to break the ill news with Old Bess standing, calm and silent, behind her, but it was. It even seemed easier for Anwara to take the blow—or else she was too dismayed to rage. She merely stood by the table and heard Saaski out, her hands motionless in the bread dough, her thin shoulders drooping. Then she sighed deeply, wiped her hands, and went to poke up the fire.

"Put away the churn, then," she said harshly. "You will bake the loaves this morning while I'm at my weeding. Don't let them burn."

"I won't, Mumma," Saaski murmured, and that was the end of it.

Later, when Anwara had gone to the Lowfield and the loaves were cooling, Old Bess came back, carrying a small cloth-wrapped bundle. "Fetch a bowl and put a little water in it," she told Saaski. "And a pinch of salt," she added when the bowl was ready.

Saaski hesitated, then found a spoon to dip the salt out of its wooden box. Salt had always stung her fingers.

"Now come along," said Old Bess.

Saaski obeyed, carefully balancing the bowl and eyeing the little bundle still tucked under Old Bess's arm. Except for old man Fiach and his dog, both dozing in a dooryard, the street was empty. From the smithy just beyond the cowshed the clang of Yanno's hammer sounded rhythmically on the still, sun-warmed air. Old Bess walked straight to the shed wall, stooped down, and opened her bundle on the ground. It was full of the leaves and stems and yellow flowers of St. John's wort. Saaski skipped hastily back, slopping the water a little.

"It will not hurt you, Saaski," Old Bess said calmly. "You need not even touch it. Just give me the bowl, then guide my hand to the mark."

She took a handful of the plant trimmings, dipped them in the salt water, and waited. Gingerly Saaski took hold of her wrist, located the half-visible rune on the wall, and placed the hand with its dripping leaves over the center. Old Bess scrubbed—this way, that way, over the whole area. After a few moments she paused. "Is it gone?"

"Nearly," Saaski told her. "A bit toward the—that edge." She pointed, holding her finger just off the wood.

Old Bess dipped a fresh handful of leaves and flowers and scrubbed again. This time nothing was left. Saaski met Old

Bess's questioning glance and nodded. *Why can I see it and you cannot?* she wanted to ask, but kept silent, fearing she might not want the answer.

"Then pour out the water, and take the bowl back to its shelf. Our little task is done." Old Bess bundled up the crushed trimmings and tied the cloth. She smiled her tight, brief smile at Saaski. "If you dream of some other rune, will you come and show me?"

"I will," Saaski murmured.

"Good. Now I'll just have a word with your da'." She turned and headed for the smithy.

A word with Yanno? What about? Uneasy again, Saaski watched from the cottage dooryard until Old Bess disappeared under the wide smithy roof and Yanno's clanging broke off. Then she darted closer, ducking behind the tall clump of gray-and-gold mullein that grew by the smithy wall. Yanno's deep voice rumbled; Old Bess's answer floated out clearly.

"Nay, I was but passing—and puzzling about your cow. I wonder, Yanno, that you do not hang a horseshoe over the door of that shed."

More rumbling, with a questioning lift at the end.

"Eh, well." Old Bess's voice had a shrug in it. "It is said to turn away bad luck. Tell Anwara I will bring her some melilot tomorrow to flavor her cheese."

Old Bess emerged from the smithy and went her way up the street. Saaski watched from behind the mullein clump, forgetting to move because of consternation about the horseshoe. Would Yanno do that? Nail iron right over the door she had to go in and out of twice a day? Iron made her shiver, made her teeth ache and hurt her if she touched it. Yanno knew it did—they all knew. Old Bess had just begun to seem so friendly—now this. There was no puzzling her out.

The clanging from the smithy started up again, but at a jerky pace, and suddenly there was the clatter of Yanno's hammer landing amid his other tools. Belatedly, Saaski came to her senses and scampered home. She was barely inside when Yanno stalked past.

A moment later the hammer blows sounded again, not ringing as they did against the anvil but with a somber *thunk, thunk, thunk* as the horseshoe was nailed above the cow byre door.

8

After the horseshoe went up there was no further trouble about the milking. And for a while, there was no other nuisance to blame Saaski for. True, she had to force herself into the shed each morning and evening, shivering as she passed under the horseshoe, but this bothered no one but her.

A far larger burden was the unused energy now bottled up inside her. Forbidden the moor and her free wanderings, she attacked the churning with a vigor that sloshed the milk out of the tall wooden churn, swept the smooth-trampled earth floor so hard she raised dust where there had been none loose before. She had a rough hand with the bread dough and washed crocks hard enough to crack them. Since she balked at scouring the iron pot—braving the horseshoe twice a day was bad enough—she was put to scrubbing the hearthstones, and the table, and Yanno's other tunic until he complained that she had well-nigh worn it out.

All this took up only part of her morning.

"It'll never answer," Old Bess had told Anwara at the outset. "You may cage her but she'll slip out through the bars—or beat herself senseless against them."

"Mother, what blather! Any child needs to learn to mind a house, and do the tasks."

"This child needs freedom. She needs the moor."

"The moor! Why, you know as well as I—" With an indignant cluck Anwara dismissed the matter. "Doesn't she go daily to gather wood? That's roaming aplenty. When the sheep shearing's done next week, I'll put her to washing my fleeces."

Saaski vigorously washed the fleeces: but she was too rough when it came to carding them, far too impatient to spin; her thread turned out full of lumps and skinny spots and could not be given to Oleg the weaver. Under Anwara's stern eye Saaski knitted it into a rather lumpy shawl for herself.

When that was done, the idleness set in again. It was not in her to sit still, or even to dawdle over tasks to make them last longer. Sometimes she slipped outside and ran around and around the cottage—still obediently "at home" but at least moving, skipping, leaping. Sometimes she simply jumped up and down in the middle of the room until she collapsed in a breathless heap. Once she climbed up onto the thatch—without a ladder—and spent a satisfying hour scrambling about, pulling tufts of wild grass off the reeds, until Anwara came back from the Lowfield and screeched with fright to see where she was—then screeched at Yanno for not keeping his eyes open, whereupon Yanno bellowed that he was a smith, not a nanny, and Anwara would henceforth take that plaguey young one along to help with the weeding, and watch her herself!

But there was a proper and time-honored way to weed the grain. One used a hooked stick to separate a weed from the grain stems, a forked stick to pin it down, and the hooked one again to uproot it as one moved step-by-step along the row, leaving a mulch as well as a path for the reaper to follow.

Saaski was not tall enough to use the weeding sticks. She went back to the cottage.

Meanwhile May was passing, and the moor was dressing itself in wildflowers, and Tam was far away on top of the world no doubt fluting and juggling all by himself. One day Saaski tied all the clothes and bedclothes in the house together just to be doing something. The next, she plucked the tail feathers out of Anwara's hens and stuck them in her hair until she looked like a new and astonishing kind of bird. Forbidden such games in Yanno's most exasperated roar, she fell at last into a silent dark dejection that began to bother her parents as much as her mischief did.

"*Now* what ails her?" Yanno demanded of Anwara one morning, grouchy with worry. "Dose her with valerian, can't you? Or coltsfoot or cowslip or—"

"She needs no quieting—she's too quiet!" Anwara snapped. "Much you know about dosing young ones."

"Well, do something! Ask your mother, then. It may be she'll know a cure."

But Anwara did not care to ask Old Bess and be told again that Saaski needed her freedom, and the moor. Instead she asked Saaski if a tooth hurt, or her stomach felt queasy, and got a blank look and an indifferent shake of the head in reply.

Saaski scarcely heard Anwara's edgy questions. She had finally begun to ask herself what was wrong with her, why she was so different from everybody else, and what would be the end of it. She found no answer, but the question weighed on her. For all she knew, answering it would be worse than all the rest.

And then one day, alone in the house with her tasks done, she climbed up to swing by her knees from a rafter to see how the room looked upside down, and noticed the door to the put-away cupboard where Anwara stowed everybody's winter cloaks and beechwood clogs when the snows were over. It was a small cupboard, tucked under the straw-fringed eaves in a dim corner of the storage loft, and easy to forget about. But Anwara had been known to bring down a pot of honey she had laid by there, and Saaski decided to explore it.

She got right side up on the rafter and scampered along it, until she could drop onto the loft and edge her way between the baskets holding straw rope and torch reeds, the spare sheepskins for winter bedding, a broken-legged stool, Anwara's soap-making cauldron. No doubt there would be only more such oddments in the cupboard, but Saaski meant to find out. Crouched on the rough boards in front of it and brushing spiderwebs away from her face, she fumbled gingerly with the latch, using a handful of her apron to protect her fingers as she tugged the iron pin out. At last the hasp grated free of its staple and the cupboard door creaked open. Sucking her fingers, which tingled in spite of the apron, Saaski peered inside.

A linen sack, beeswaxed at the seams, turned out to be half full of the goose down Anwara was storing for new pillows. Behind it, a stiffened sheep-hide pouch held nothing but a broken knife. There were the winter togs, and a pot of red earth for Anwara's dyes—no honey crocks, though. In fact, nothing else, except—far back in the gloom—a dim bundle of something wrapped carefully in sheepskin, fleece side in. Saaski stretched an arm to its longest, tugged the bundle into reach and began to lay back its coverings, sneezing from the dust. Inside the fleece was some other kind of sheep-hide pouch, empty and flat but feeling still supple under an exploring finger, and on top of it—indeed, attached to it, she could see now—were several long, thin, gangly, jointed, black, nickle-trimmed, ivory-capped, tubular, tasseled . . .

It was a set of bagpipes.

Joy swept like a gale through Saaski. Breathless and bubble light, she pounced on the pipes and scrambled backward along the loft, dragging them with her, heedless of the baskets she upset or the clatter she made. Perched like a bird on the rafter again, with feet braced wide, she located the blowpipe and puffed vigorously into it until her eyes felt crossed, with little effect on the bag, which hung at her side, still maddeningly slim and sleeping—though not quite flat. She rested a moment, then drew in a prodigious breath and blew again, at the same time giving the bag a clout that helped it awake and swell, and drew the first startled sob from the drones. Tucking the inflated bag firmly under her arm, and blowing steadily, she swung the three drones over her shoulder. Her hands found the chanter and her fingers the holes along its sides with only a little fumbling, and settled into a position they already knew. Then the shrill, shrieking cry of the chanter shattered the quiet of the afternoon, running up and down and around the scale in a wild little air soon accompanied, as the drones warmed up, by a three-voiced groaning, high and low, on a single sonorous note. The tune had not ended before it swerved into another, more frenzied and clamorous than the first, which rollicked and frolicked around the little house and out over the village with a noise to wake the dead.

Yanno's was the first shocked face to appear in the doorway. He stared frantically around, then up. Stumbling into the room, he stood motionless, his wide, disbelieving gaze fixed on the rafter. At his heels several children crowded into the open door; behind them old Fiach blinked; Helsa the wife of Alun craned and hopped trying to see around Fiach. Saaski paid no heed, only finished her rigadoon to start a pibroch of a high, piercing sweetness that had her listeners clutching their ears in pain. It was one thing to hear bagpipes wailing and groaning across the moor; in the confines of a little room it was quite another.

Yanno regained his power of speech. "Come down from there! Stop that and come down!" he roared, but could not be heard over the racket. Several more faces appeared at the doorway and one or two peered through the tiny window. Saaski was ending her pibroch when the cluster of villagers shifted in confusion, then parted to admit Anwara, and after her, Old Bess. Anwara hurried across the room toward Yanno and like him, froze, staring up at the rafter. Old Bess took one long, astonished, comprehending look, then began firmly herding the gaping visitors out of the cottage. She latched the door and placed her own tall person in front of the window as Saaski, giddy with excitement, began an ear-splitting fanfare.

When it was finished, she paused for breath. The silence was almost as stunning as the noise had been.

The first to recover, Yanno gasped, "Come down, you imp!" His voice shook, and he paused to swallow. "Put those pipes back, d'you hear me? And *come you down* from there!"

The glorious, wondrous, joyful afternoon shattered around Saaski. She focused at last on his outraged face, glimpsed Anwara's dazed one beside him, and realized there was going to be another argle-bargle. Maybe the worst yet, because she knew already she was not going to obey. She did not move, except to tighten her clutch on the pipes. The silence rang in her ears.

Into it, Anwara spoke, her eyes dark with a bewilderment that, like Yanno's, seemed close to fright. "Child, how in God's earth did you learn to play the pipes?"

Relaxing a bit with her own surprise, Saaski transferred her gaze to Anwara. She could not comprehend the question. "Learn?" she repeated.

"Aye, learn! It's plain enough you have learned, somehow or other! Who was't taught you?"

Saaski could only shake her head in confusion and

growing anxiety. Again, she had done something that seemed to her perfectly natural, but to others, strange. "Nobody taught me."

"But you were playing them!"

No use denying that. "I was. They were made for playing. Can you not play them yourself?" Saaski ventured.

"I?" Anwara laughed sharply. "No more than I can breathe underwater! And it's the same for your da'!"

"But the pipes were *here*—in the put-away cupboard just yonder—" Saaski let go the chanter long enough to point an exasperated finger. Where there were pipes there was surely someone to play them; anything else was witless.

Yanno spoke heavily. "The pipes were my da's. He was a champion piper, he was. But I'll have no young one fidgetin' about with my da's pipes, and mebbe leavin' 'em out in the wet, or—"

"I'd never do so!" Saaski exclaimed.

"Nonetheless—," said Yanno, overriding her. "You'll put 'em back now where they belong and climb down from there!"

Saaski only folded her arms tighter about the pipes. This time she was not going to be scared, and she was not going to be obedient. She was going to stay on this rafter until she starved and fell off it, rather than put the pipes back in that cupboard. They did *not* belong there. They belonged *here*, in her hands, under her arm, pressing into her left shoulder. And here they would stay.

"Saaski—!" roared Yanno.

Anwara spoke up. "Hold your peace, husband. She's not

hurting the pipes. Did you not hear how she can play? And without teaching." She hesitated, then declared, "'Tis a gift from God."

"Or from the Devil," Yanno retorted.

"Blather!" retorted Anwara—a little too swiftly. Their eyes held a moment, then she turned away. Wearily, she added, "Let the child have them. It's the first time I've seen her smile in a fortnight."

"She'll make more mischief!" Yanno protested.

Old Bess spoke suddenly from her post near the window. "More likely, the pipes will keep her from it. Come, Yanno—of what use to anyone are they in that cupboard?"

Outnumbered and beginning to be out-argued, Yanno clutched at a final straw. "But they're my da's own pipes!"

"Aye, but your da' can't play them, can he?" Anwara flung at him. "He's gone to his reward—that's if the good Lord saw fit to reward him for a life spent three-quarters drunken! And *you* can't play a pennywhistle. So let be! Stick to your anvil and leave the child her tunes!"

"*Achh*, well-an'-all," Yanno growled, glaring from one to another of them like a thwarted bear. "What's a man to do, with the three of you females all agin 'im! I wash my hands of it!" He stalked to the door and slammed out of it, still muttering.

Saaski, hugging her precious bagpipes and feeling her whole face lift and crease in a grin of triumph, was conscious of an odd and new emotion as she fixed her gaze on Anwara. It was joy—but it was more. She was still trying to name it, to fathom it, when Anwara walked forward and reached up, saying, "Hand me the pipes and then come

84

down from there. You'll be the death of me with your antics! What if you'd fallen?"

"I won't fall, Mumma," said Saaski, but she jumped down at once, brushing the dust from her petticoats without anyone telling her, then stood searching Anwara's face, still trying to puzzle out the new feeling. She wished Anwara would give her a fiercely hard task to do, or walk into terrible danger so she could rush to the rescue. She felt a strong need to repay.

But Anwara merely handed her the pipes, said, "Find a safe place to keep them. And mind you don't neglect your tasks to sit playing all day long."

"I won't! I vow I won't!" said Saaski fervently, and at that moment she meant every word.

9

But it was one thing to promise, another to keep faith, with the bagpipes always tempting her to neglect her tasks or hurry through them skimble-skamble, just to be done and free to make tunes.

She kept the pipes in the truckle bed woven of straw-rope that she had slept in as an infant, pushed under the low cot she slept in now, and out of sight. But they were in her mind's eye all the same, and the tunes ran through her head, pushing and joggling to get out. She could seldom resist dropping her work to fetch out the pipes, fill the bag, and give them voice.

Of all who heard them—and not one of the eighty-seven men, women, children, and infants in the village could avoid hearing them, including old Fiach, who was half-deaf—only Yanno's sister Ebba thoug[ht to ask the] question: "What tunes are those?"

Nobody could answer it. Everybody bega[n to talk about] it. Nobody had ever heard those tunes bef[ore; they were] nothing like the old traditional ones that ev[erybody grew] up knowing, the ones Yanno's da' had use[d to] play. So where had Saaski learned them? Ebba's question became the focus of the gossip around the village well. Helsa the wife of Alun put it to Anwara, who stared at her a moment and said, "Likely she makes them up."

Nobody believed that. Inevitably, somebody brought up the Elf King's Tune—said to be music so strange, so wild and compelling that even the trees and stones were forced to dance. But nobody had seen any trees or stones kicking up their heels. They backed off a bit, turning it over in their minds as they filled their buckets.

"All the same," Ebba summed it up as they prepared to part, "no young one could make such tunes up out of her head. There's something about 'em not rightly 'uman. That's what I say."

"And what I've been saying these ten years!" put in Helsa, with her eyebrows raised and her smile thin. She lowered her voice; the others leaned toward her in a huddle of head kerchiefs. "A changeling she is, or I've never eat pease porridge! And what'll come of it if we don't do something, I hate to say."

"But what can we do?" whispered young Cattila, rather timidly, into a silence.

Nobody cared to answer.

that moment the peace of the afternoon, filled only with the bees' humming and a medley of birdsong, was broken by the all-too-familiar initial choking sob of the drones. The birds fell silent as one of the weirder, wilder tunes rose out of the smith's cottage and filled the street. It was soon accompanied by the wails of village infants rudely wakened from their afternoon naps, as well as the howling of old Fiach's dog.

"*One* thing we can do is get shut of that racket and ruction!" said Ebba in her normal loud and angry voice. "I say send that creetur back up to the moor she likes so well! I doubt there's any danger for one like her."

"And if there is," Helsa slid in, "then so be it. There'll be nothing left for *us* to do."

Heads nodded—thoughtfully, then firmly. Cattila ventured, "But who will tell Anwara?"

"I'll tell Yanno," Ebba snapped, picking up her buckets. "It'll be a fine day when I'm afeard of my own brother!"

As she and everyone knew, it would be an even finer one when Yanno heeded much she said. But by this time Yanno was as tired of his decree that Saaski should bide in the cottage as he was flummoxed by how to reverse himself. Outargued in the matter of his da's bagpipes, he could not bring himself to back down on another matter, too.

Then something else happened. One midmorning when everybody was busy with flocks or fields or indoor tasks, old Fergil the fisherman walked down the deserted village street to the smithy. Yanno blinked a moment before he recognized the hulking, stooped figure silhouetted against the brightness of the wide doorway. Rarely did Fergil leave his lonely hut among the dunes between Moor Water and the sea to venture near his fellow creatures. Only when need drove him to replace his much-patched boots or his supply of fishhooks and eel traps did he come into the village, and then when it was all but empty.

"So, Fergil," said Yanno, putting aside the iron rim he was fitting to the wooden blade of a spade. "Hooks, is it? Or did one of the traps I made you break?"

Fergil shook his shaggy head as he stepped into the shade of the smithy. "Traps good," he muttered. His voice was rusty with disuse.

"I make them to last," remarked Yanno. "Then 'tis hooks you're after. Which size are you needing?"

"Handful of the little 'uns. Ten or so big 'uns for the one-eyes and the saumon."

"That'll be more than a moment's work, man. I've this spade and another to finish and both Edildan's oxen to shoe afore I can get to it, even. Call it a se'nnight."

"Aye, well." Fergil shifted his feet a bit. "Can y' bring 'em?"

"What, bring 'em clean down there t'other side of Moor Water? Fergil, come fetch 'em. I'm a busy man, friend."

"Can't rightly get away," Fergil mumbled, beginning to edge toward the door and dart suspicious glances into the shadows behind the forge.

Can but won't, thought Yanno, irritation struggling as usual with pity for the strange old fellow. Sighing, he was about to give in as he always did with Fergil when it occurred to him that Saaski was old enough by now to send on errands. "Aye, well, then—," he began. The rest was lost in the sudden cough and moan of the drones starting up next door, followed by the chanter's cry soaring wild into the morning.

Fergil's eyes opened wide and rolled toward the wall separating cottage and smithy; he stumbled back and seemed about to bolt. Yanno shouted a reassurance; before he could finish, the fisherman suddenly went as still as some carved image of himself, his gaze fixed intently on the wall. The sounds coming through it had now resolved themselves into one of Saaski's piercing, curious little tunes.

Fergil moved not a muscle until it ended. Then he whispered hoarsely, "Who plays those pipes?"

"Nobbut my daughter," Yanno told him, trying to brush the subject away. "A child only—she knows no proper tunes."

Fergil gave him a strange, long look. "That's never a child of yours, Yanno. Never. No."

"What're you saying, man?" growled Yanno, forced almost to roar it because another tune had started from beyond the wall.

"That's no child playin', no. No." Fergil could barely be heard but his head was shaking back and forth, his eyes glassy, his meaning plain.

"Come, then, I'll show you," cried Yanno, keeping a wary eye on the man as he grasped his arm to urge him out of the smithy. Fergil was such an odd one, nobody knew what he might do.

However he did nothing but allow himself to be guided

90

outside and around to the cottage dooryard. Yanno threw open the door and gestured. There was Saaski, perched on her rafter, piping, while below her, Anwara set the loaves to the fire.

Fergil stood, wooden, staring at Saaski, unheeding when Anwara arose from the hearth with a quick glance at Yanno and said good day. Yanno demanded, "Will y' believe, now?" but Fergil was deaf to him, too.

Only when Saaski abruptly broke off her tune and met his fixed look with a curious one did Fergil edge backward, past Yanno. He was still wooden-faced, but shaking in every limb.

"Can't you see it's nobbut my little one?" Yanno asked, exasperated because Fergil was making him acutely uneasy the more he stared.

"No," muttered Fergil. "No. No. No. No. No." He whirled suddenly and made off down the street, never slowing nor glancing to right or left until he plunged into the woods and out of sight.

"Poor old lackbrain!" Anwara muttered to Yanno as they stood together in the doorway. "What ails him now?" Her voice was casual but she was tensely searching his face.

Yanno shrugged his big shoulders as if he would shrug the whole morning off, the whole week, maybe the whole past uneasy eleven years. It often struck him that life had been sadder but simpler, childless. "Likely vexed by the sound of pipes," he growled. "Or maychance it's the plaguey tunes she plays on 'em! Where in the name o' Old Clootie does she get 'em, anyway?"

"She makes 'em up," said Anwara sharply, crossing herself

at mention of the Devil. "Don't you, child?" she added as she turned back into the house.

Saaski, still blinking over the odd behavior of the stranger and hoping it had nothing much to do with her, barely heard the question until Anwara repeated it, insistently.

"You make the tunes up, don't you? Outa your own head?"

For an impatient moment Saaski focused on the matter. It seemed to her she had always known those tunes. But maybe she made them up. "I dunno. Who was that man?" she asked Anwara.

"Oh. Nobody." Anwara abruptly busied herself with the waterbucket. "Just old Fergil the fisherman. Come down now, I want you to mind the loaves."

"He stared at me."

"Aye, well, he's a bit touched, poor man. Some say he was hexed, long ago. Come you down, I must go to the well. And put away those pipes!"

Reluctantly Saaski descended, tucked the bagpipes into their trundle bed, and settled herself beside the hearth as Anwara picked up the bucket, plucked her blue shawl from its peg, and hastily left the house.

Doesn't want to talk about that man, Saaski thought, looking after her—and grew more curious than before.

Yanno had already gone back to his anvil and the spade rim, on which he was venting some of his baffled spleen with ringing hammer blows.

It was now plain to him: the child and her piping had to be got out of the village and as far out of earshot as he could manage, before he harmed her or his da's pipes, one or the other. But he could not back down about the moor.

By next noonday he had worked out a face-saving compromise. Nowadays the cows were pastured in the wasteland above the Highfield, to let the grass in the lower meadows grow for hay. He thought about this. And when Anwara came as usual to bring him his ale, complaining about the bagpipes caterwauling in her ears half the day, he was ready for her.

"Now, you're not to worry your poor achin' head about it, wife. I'll see to everything," he told her expansively. "We'll strike a bargain with the child, that's what we'll do," he said as if he had only just thought of it, instead of tossing and fretting half the night. "She'll take the cow each day up to the summer pasture, and do her pipin' there, and only there. 'Tisn't the moor, but it's next and nigh it, and she won't wake the babies from that far off."

So the following day Saaski was abruptly freed from her tether, to her delight and everybody else's profound relief. She did not ask what had brought about the change. But as she followed Moll up the winding hillside trail by the apple orchard that first pearly morning she was thinking Anwara must have had a hand in it, maybe Old Bess, too, as it was they she had to thank for the pipes themselves. Again she felt the new, strong urge to reciprocate—to give back joy for joy.

10

It was easy to know what would please Old Bess—there were herbs growing in the wasteland that did not thrive lower down, and strong though she was for her years, Old Bess made this climb only when she had to. Saaski kept her eyes open as she went, noting a clump of this and a patch of that, and when Moll was settled to her browsing and the bagpipes warmed up enough to send their first wild, satisfying strains across the hillside, she walked and piped, walked and piped, still searching with her eyes among the rocks and heather clumps for plants she did not see near the village.

The pipes sounded fine, up here in the high, misty morning—much finer than in the cottage, where every note rebounded off the enclosing walls and jarred against every other. It was halfway to noon before she finally blew herself out and was ready to go home. Then she picked samplings of everything she had spotted, including a fistful of red-and-white daisies for Anwara, tied the herbs in her apron, and danced her way down.

Her tasks awaited her, along with a few sharp questions from Anwara to make sure she had not slipped away to the dangerous moor.

"I stayed near the cows, Mumma," Saaski assured her, holding out the little bunch of daisies as a peace offering, though now she thought of it, she had never seen flowers in the cottage, and wondered belatedly if she'd broken a rule.

Anwara herself seemed uncertain how to react. She stared at the slightly wilting daisies and said, "Posies, is it? I always thought them better left to grow." She glanced at Saaski, and added, "Well-a-day, you meant it kindly. Dip some water into that mug with the broken handle, they'll maybe last the day. Then put away those pipes and get to your churning—the morning's near gone."

Saaski did as she was bid. Clearly, daisies were not the proper thank-you for Anwara. She would have to think of something else.

It was otherwise with Old Bess's gift. When she had washed the butter and put away the churn, Saaski scampered up the grassy street with her bundle of wasteland herbs to the little hut at the far end. It was the last house in the village, set apart from Oleg the weaver's by a thicket of hawthorn—blooming white now and scenting the sunny midday air. Beyond Old Bess's thatch the street meandered off as a narrow track winding upward across a part of the moor Saaski had not explored, and eventually toward the town. She stood a moment, gazing, wondering where Tam and his goats were now, before she stepped onto the flagstone doorstep and knocked.

"Come in, Saaski," called Old Bess as calmly as if she could see straight through the door.

Saaski obeyed, only briefly surprised. Old Bess knew all sorts of things, and never said how she knew them. This day, however, she had not guessed Saaski's errand.

"Well, child? Have you remembered another rune to show me?"

Saaski hesitated. She had seen several since that one on the cow byre; some mystifying, others suddenly familiar, their meaning plain as a shout—though how or when she had learned it she could not guess. There was one on the mill's great wheel that meant "Danger." Another on Faeren and Guthwic's root cellar, near a loose board Guthwic let go unmended, meant something like "Help yourself." Another she knew glimmered on the doorpost she had just slipped past. However, for answer she merely handed Old Bess her bundled up apron.

"What's this? Bless me! Lady's mantle. And hearts-ease—costmary . . . coltsfoot! Where did you find that, child? It's the best ever for my cough. And true chamomile—that will ease old Fiach's aching knee . . ."

She knew every leaf and sprig Saaski had brought, knew their uses. Setting Saaski to plucking the yellow-and-white flowers off the spidery chamomile, she tied the rest of the herbs in bunches to join others hanging from the rafters to dry.

Her single room was like a strange, shadowy little bower,

aromatic with a mixture of pungent smells—and a shelf near the scoured wooden table held four large, mysterious books that had belonged to Brother Oswic, the wandering monk who had once lived here. They were unlike anything Saaski had ever seen; much in Old Bess's cottage was unlike anybody else's. She was half scared of the place, wholly fascinated. But it was only since the day Old Bess had helped her scrub the rune marks from the cowshed door that she had ventured to come here on her own.

While Old Bess spread the chamomile blossoms on a net to hang like an airy hammock above the hearth, Saaski edged closer to the books, trying to imagine what secrets they held, and how one found out. They were mostly secrets about herbs, Old Bess had told her, set down by Brother Oswic and added to by Old Bess herself on the pages he had left blank.

Old Bess, as usual, read her thoughts. "Would you like to see my books?" She lifted one down, untied the thongs that bound the boards, and spread the book open on the table. The time-spotted vellum pages were covered with thin scratchings, which meant as little to Saaski as those Anwara's hens made in the dust. But here and there in the corner of a page was a little brownish drawing of a leaf, a flower, a whole plant, looking as natural as when growing in the woods.

"Silverweed," said Saaski in surprise, putting a finger on one of them.

"Yes, Brother Oswic's hand was gifted," Old Bess told her. "All his wisdom is in here, on these pages." As Saaski touched the marks, she went on, "Writing makes pictures in the mind—like runes. He taught me to read the letters. Here—look. This says, 'Silverweed eases fever. A pinch of the herb; pour boiling water over; strain through a cloth. Drink a cupful each day.'"

Saaski stared, astonished, at the marks. Runes meant only such simple things as "Keep away" or "Here it is safe." Real writing was magic. "Could I learn to read them?" she asked.

"You could. In time." Old Bess hesitated, glancing at Saaski thoughtfully. "It may be you could learn quicker than I did."

"I could? Why?"

Old Bess hesitated even longer. Saaski could not imagine what she was thinking, but it made her sky-blue eyes go darker and grayer, as if they had clouded over. And in the end she decided not to say it. Instead she took a breath, beckoned Saaski close to her, and pointed at one mark in the book. "Look. That is a letter, and its name is A. Trace it for me with your finger, there, on the table."

Saaski did so. Old Bess smiled a little, and said, "Aye, so I thought. Fetch me that piece of slate yonder on the shelf. You'll find a lump of redstone in the cup beside it."

An hour later, when Old Bess rose and took her shawl from its peg and her root basket from the hearth, the slate was scrawled with red marks and Saaski knew her letters— Old Bess told her so.

"I can read now?" she asked eagerly.

"No. You have learned twenty-six letters. You have yet to learn even one word of the many they can make. Come tomorrow and we will make some words."

Saaski watched her return the book to the shelf. She did

not want to stop, or leave the big books without knowing what was in them. "Are Brother Oswic's secrets all about curing people?"

"No. He knew many other things as well." She glanced at Saaski. "He knew some of the runes."

Startled, Saaski met her eyes. "He could see them? Like me?" *Then I would not be the only one*, she was thinking, with a relief tinged with a faint, curious sense of loss. The runes—even the mention of them—always made her feel two ways at once.

"He could not. No more than I," Old Bess said calmly.

"Then how—"

"He would never tell me how he learned about them. Or who taught him what they meant."

Saaski slowly tied on her crumpled apron, studying Old Bess's unreadable face, feeling the secret strong tug of attraction mixed with wariness that runes and certain bird-songs and those faint, curious streaks on the moor always roused in her. "But he taught *you*?"

"Well-a-day, he taught me what he knew. But I learned more from the gypsies."

Saaski stared in astonishment. "Gypsies? The ones who pass this way each year?"

"Very like them. A different band. They brought me to this village, long ago."

"You are a *gypsy*?"

Old Bess smiled, and shook her head. She set her shawl and root basket aside and sat down again, pulling Saaski down beside her on the hearth bench. "No, child—only a foundling. The gypsies came across me at a crossroads somewhere in the south country—a newborn lying in a seed basket. They thought at first I was nobbut a bit of sheepskin, then they saw different and near drowned me as some outcast from a pixie's nest. Or so my good Milligren used to tell me—when she would tell me anything about it. She took me in, I never knew why, and raised me with her other young ones till I was near your age. And when finally the band roamed northward they left me here in Torskaal in the dead of one midnight, asleep in my truckle bed outside the miller's gate, with the same sheepskin over me, and the seed basket beside me. When dawn came, Guin the miller's grandda', who was miller then, found me there. But my gypsies were long gone."

"Why? Why did they leave you?" Saaski whispered. Her eyes felt wide enough to pop from her head. "Why did they leave the sheepskin and the basket?"

Old Bess shrugged. "The sheepskin was like those of the sheep you see hereabouts, shaggy and long haired, not a mat of curls like a southland sheep. And the basket was like any Torskaal man uses when he sows his fields. Perhaps they thought I belonged here."

"Do *you* think so?" Saaski asked softly.

"I have sometimes wondered if I belong anywhere," Old Bess told her.

After a moment tangled with feelings she could not name, Saaski whispered, "I, too. Leastwise—if I do—I think it is not Torskaal." *Yet how can that be, when I have never been anywhere else?* she asked herself, or meant to, but realized she had spoken aloud, asking Old Bess, too. She stared earnestly into the woman's weathered face, hoping—half expecting—to find the answer. But she could no more read it there than she could so far read the secrets in the books.

Abruptly Old Bess rose, reaching for her shawl. "Aye, well, Guin the miller's grandda' took me in; I was raised with his brood and married his eldest, who died of a pox when Anwara was half grown. By then old Brother Oswic had settled in this house, and I came each day and swept and cooked for him, and learned from him until he died. When Anwara wed I moved out of the miller's house at last and came to live here, for I like well to be alone." She picked up her root basket and led the way to the door. "And here I am still."

The stories and the moment of closeness were over, at least for today. Reluctantly Saaski followed Old Bess out the door, remembered the rune she had seen on it when she came, and turned back quickly. The marks were still there, fading and shimmering by turns. She touched Old Bess's arm and pointed to them.

"I have one now?" Old Bess peered hard at the wood, but shook her head. "I cannot see it."

Saaski drew it in the dirt of the pathway with her toe.

"What does it mean, child? Do you know?"

"It means 'Keep away,'" Saaski told her, with a little grin.

Old Bess smiled, then gave her brief, rare laugh. "So. I am safe from mischief, am I? For a time, anyway."

Whose mischief? Saaski wondered, as they started together along the street. Who makes the marks? Why do I know them—some of them—and what they mean?

She had no idea of the answer. But the questions

101

themselves had roused in her the familiar restlessness, the confused feelings of yearning and loss, that had plagued her since she could remember. The only cure was the pipes, and playing them long and loud. When they reached the blacksmith's cottage she skipped in, leaving Old Bess to press on with her quest for roots and mushrooms. With luck, Anwara was up in the Lowfield, or tending the hens, or . . .

But Anwara was there, a hank of brown fleece on her shoulder, fingers busy with the drop-spindle as she paced from hearth to cupboard and back again. A new-spun skein lay on the table, half hiding the little bunch of red-and-white daisies, still slightly drooping, in their mug.

Saaski eyed the flowers, dissatisfied. She would have to do better.

"You have been long with my mother," Anwara remarked with a penetrating look. "If you went there, indeed!"

"I did! She showed me her books."

"Showed you her books?" Anwara's voice was astonished; her fingers missed their catch and the spindle fell dangling and twirling, unwinding the arm's length of thread she had just wound on it. Saaski pounced, captured it, and returned it. Absently Anwara wound up the thread again, her surprised gaze still on Saaski. "Well-and-all! I'm sure she never showed *me* any of them." The spindle began its smooth down-and-up motion and her fingers their rhythmic dance as she added, "Not that I ever plagued her to look at them—great, dusty bundles—whatever would I think to see?"

Maybe, thought Saaski, that is why she never showed you them.

Yet she herself had not plagued or even asked, just

looked—and wished—and Old Bess had known it. Perhaps Old Bess knew everything. Everything in the world. Except not all the runes.

Anwara resumed her spinning-walk. When her back was turned, Saaski tugged the old trundle bed from under her cot and snatched out the bagpipes.

"I'll fetch the cow now, Mumma," she sang out, already halfway to the door.

"Now? It's not time yet!"

But Saaski was gone. Anwara caught her spindle and came to the doorway. The sun was but halfway down toward the great shoulder of the hills. Angrily she called Saaski back to gather eggs and scrub the hearth. By then Saaski was nowhere to be seen.

Aware of amused glances from neighboring doorways—nobody else's children could disappear so fast—Anwara clamped her vexation between her teeth and turned back into the house.

A moment later, Saaski slithered down the far side of an apple tree, hitched the pipes to her shoulder, and hurried on up the path toward the wasteland—and the moor beyond. Forbidden or not, she was going straight there. Maybe if she did not tell anybody, nobody would ask—or really care—how far she strayed. . . . Except Anwara. Anwara always asked. But perhaps she would lie to Anwara. Or just—not answer.

It no longer mattered. She had to go back to the moor. She could no longer stay away from the only place she had ever felt she belonged.

PART III

11

When Saaski was willing to mind—which was most of the time—she was as biddable as any other village child. When she had decided to balk, nothing could move her. Anwara might scold, Yanno might thunder and even raise his great blacksmith's hand, though he could never bring himself to strike her. She remained passive, her strange eyes mirror-dark and her pointed face sad. But once her household tasks were done, she waited only till Anwara glanced away, then she was gone. Short of tying her to the doorpost, they could no longer keep her off the moor.

"Let her be, Daughter," Old Bess counseled, stopping by the cottage one day to find Anwara in frustrated tears. "I have told you. She will come to no harm on the moor."

"She should do as she's bid!" cried Anwara.

"She does so—in everything but this." Old Bess watched

107

as Anwara dashed a hand across her eyes and angrily blew her nose. "It is the moor itself you fear, is it not?" When Anwara did not answer, she took off her shawl, laid her little gift of sweet cicely on the table, and said coaxingly, "Come, brew us a cup and sit awhile, and calm yourself. Saaski will come back. But she cannot help going, and you'd best make your peace with it."

Anwara's shoulders drooped, and she did not answer, only pushed the kettle over the fire on its iron arm, and crumbled dried mint into a pot. They did not mention the matter again.

However, after that day she did not forbid Saaski to go where she would, or complain to Yanno. Yanno was glad to let the subject drop, to turn his mind back to his smithing, which he knew something about, and tell himself the two of them must have worked it out somehow.

It was a vast relief for Saaski. Her life had already begun to be two lives—the humdrum one in the village, made irksome by the bedevilment of the other children, though brightened by Old Bess and the books—and the other, truant life, high among the mists and bogs and wild, stony reaches of the moor. She was never sure which part of the moor she liked best—the steep broom-gilded, heather-shadowed slopes always solid underfoot, or the sometimes steeper bogs, spiced with danger. After a dry spell a bog was merely a mat of thready, springy moss that you could bound across as if your feet had sprouted little wings. In wet weather—which was scarier but exciting—you had to pick your way across a bog, wary of the tall tussocks of sedge and cotton grass that marked the wettest spots, where a misstep could set you sinking and struggling into the sucking depths. But the glimmering little tracks she often saw there always traced a safe pathway—though she was careful never to put a foot directly on that glimmer.

The tracks crisscrossed the dry moor, too. Now and then she fancied she saw something—or someone—scurrying along them, too small to be a man, too moor-skilled to be a lost child, a shape moving too erratically to focus on. But if she managed a closer look, it always turned out to be a moorhen after all, or the flitting shadow of a raven wheeling overhead—or nothing but fancy.

She had soon found Tam and the goats again, by climbing as high as she could and listening for the mellow, fluttering sound of shepherd's pipes and the tinkle of Divil's bell.

"So! You've come back at last!" Tam exclaimed the day she first showed herself—a bit hesitantly—around the shoulder of the big rock he was leaning against. "I reckoned you'd changed your mind and didn't like us after all." His eyes widened as she stepped into full view. "What's *that* you've got? It's never bagpipes! Can you play 'em?"

"I can," Saaski told him, grinning at his surprise and tucking the bag under her arm. "Will we play together?"

"We will! But this reed's got too soft a voice—I'd best use me wee screamer." Tam tucked away his long reed pipe and got out the small one hollowed from a finger-thick twig. "So give us a tune! I'll find if I can tootle along o' you."

Saaski huffed and puffed the bag full, turning hot-faced with the effort, gave it the little clout with her fist that produced its preliminary coughing wail, then launched into

109

one of the liveliest of her strange little tunes. Tam listened a moment, his mouth ajar, once lifted his little pipe to his lips but then lowered it again and sat bemused till she'd finished.

"I'll never learn *that'n* just tootlin' along," he told her. "Who taught it to you, Hizzoner the Elf King?"

"Nobody taught me," Saaski retorted, her bright day suddenly dimming. "You making game of me?"

"I'm not, then!" he said promptly. "That's a magic music if ever I heard any. And I suspicion I *have* heard some, now and again, out here on this moor." He looked away, over the waste of rocks and heather and towering cloud pillars, his three goats nibbling in the foreground, and far behind them a gray, narrow curtain of rain brushing the horizon.

Following his gaze, Saaski could see only her familiar playground, the one place where she need not guard her tongue and mind her ways. Perhaps that was magic, in a way—but not in the way Tam meant. She said, "*You* tootle a bit, then, and I'll see can *I* follow."

Tam was willing, and after a few blunderings Saaski caught his rhythm and began to play along, over and under his little pipe's shrill melody like a bramble vine twining a sapling. Next, her bagpipes became a tree—a sonorous, solemn drone-song with the chanter wailing, and Tam twined it with brambly whistlings. Well pleased with themselves, they stopped to get their breath and follow the goats over a rise. From here they could see, nestled in the next hollow, the tinker's little two-wheeled cart with its raggedy hood, and next to it a reed hut of the sort shepherds build, with an ox skin roofing the space between. The pony grazed at its tether a little distance away; the old dog drowsed by a cart wheel.

"Bruman is there?" asked Saaski. "He is making the shoes and boots and leathern things?"

"Sleeping it off, more likely."

Saaski rolled her eyes at him. Old Bess had no good word for drunkards—including Yanno's dead pipe-playing da'—nor did Anwara. Saaski had never seen one, that she knew of—only the village men getting merry on a feast day, or coming unsteadily home in the dusk from Sorcha the alewife's, up near the mill.

Tam laughed at her, showing the little gap at the side of his grin. "Eh, well, that's Bruman. He mended a leathern bucket for an old fisher t'other day and got paid in muxta, so what else could he do but set to and drink it up? He's been worse lately," Tam added, the smile fading. "It's his leg, I reckon. Pains him somethin' fierce now-days. So he drinks hisself blind. One day he'll stumble into a bog and that's the last anybody'll see of him. I told 'im so, t'other day! Right to his face, I did."

"Whad'he say?" asked Saaski, wide-eyed.

"Eh—just growled at me." Tam glanced away, shrugging. "Said the bog sounded right restful. Said he'd make shift to find one and step in! Aye, sure. *Then* what'd me and the pony and goats and ol' Warrior do with ourselves, I wonder?"

Saaski had no answer, but he did not seem to expect one. "What's he look like—Bruman?" she asked, finding her mental image becoming too odd to be convincing.

"Just a whiskery, rough-lookin' fella," said Tam in surprise.

111

"Limps, y'know, leans on that crutch he made for hisself. I'll show you. Tomorrow, next day, he'll be back in his senses. Come up and I'll take you to see him."

But a day or two later, when Saaski climbed to the goats' grazing place, she had a different question on her mind. She and Tam piped a few tunes together, then the mist turned to rain and they had to pull up their hoods and huddle in the lee of an outcrop until it stopped. It seemed a good time to talk. "You know a fisherman called Fergil?" she asked Tam.

Tam glanced at her oddly. "Not rightly, no. Not meself. But Bruman does a job for 'im now and again. 'Twas Fergil paid 'im in muxta last week." He paused, scanning her face. "A-course I've heard tell of 'im. Haven't you?"

Instead of answering, she asked another question. "What've you heard tell of him?"

"Same as you, likely. He's a lack-witted old hermit, like. They do say he turned up outa nowhere one winter, long ago, wanderin' the moor without even a cloak on. Folks say he'd likely follered the fool's-fire, lost his way. Never been right in his head since. Harmless, though." Tam shrugged, added curiously, "What put you in mind of him, then?"

"Eh—I dunno," Saaski murmured. She did know, well enough. But just now she was busy comparing what Tam had told her with the little she'd already heard. "He came to our cottage, once when I was piping. Stood there gapin' at me, then took off down the street like the bukka were after him."

But yesterday midday Yanno had put a cloth-wrapped packet on the table in front of Saaski and said it was Fergil's fishhooks, and she was to take them and get his coppers for

112

the work. She'd jumped up quickly, but Anwara frowned at him and added, "If you're not afeard?"

"Whatever would I be afeard of?" she'd asked blankly. So then she'd gone a long walk down through the woods to Moor Water and around the reedy shore, to Fergil's little stone house and cow byre set back among the dunes on the other side. She'd been glad to go, curious about the noddikins, resolved to ask him straight out if he'd been hexed.

But she'd never got next or nigh him. His dog came out and barked at her before she'd set foot in his dooryard, and instead of hushing it he just yelled over its racket for her to put the fishhooks in the mug beside the manger, and find the coppers there. On her way to the byre she'd looked back to find him out of his door, holding the dog now but staring after her. Indeed he'd waved her on, shaking his shaggy head and bellowing, "No. No. I want nothin' to do with the likes o' you!"

Now here was Tam's story sounding quite different from Anwara's. "Will we go see Bruman today?" she asked after a moment.

Tam gave her his teasing grin, made somehow jauntier by the little gap. "He knows no more of that fisherman than I do."

"I never said—"

"Didn't need to. Come along, he's as sober as he ever gets. Ask him all you've a mind to. He loves to talk—when he's in the mood."

Bruman was a whiskery, rough-looking fellow, as Tam had told her, and at first seemed nothing more. He sat hunched at his workbench under the tattered ox hide stretched between cart hood and hut thatch—a big-shouldered, thin-shanked, middle-aged man in a worn leathern tunic, with his left leg extended stiffly before him. Gray streaked his wiry hair and a deep furrow carved each cheek, but there was vigor in the bloodshot glance he threw at Saaski as they approached. His hands paused on the soft boot he was patching, then went on of themselves, as his eyes lingered on Saaski. What he thought of her she could not tell. Her own gaze kept returning to the crutch lying beside him, a stout limb of beech fitted with a leather-padded crosspiece, both dark with use.

The old dog, Warrior, struggled up from his place by the cartwheel and padded stiffly forward to greet and sniff them both. Tam ruffled the dog's ears, and it sat down heavily on his foot. "I brought me friend from the village," he told Bruman. "Her name's Saaski."

"Yanno the smith's young one," Bruman said in a husky, rattly voice that sounded as if mice had been at it. He cleared his throat, harrumphed a time or two. "Heard of you, I have."

"Aye, well, she's heard o' you, too, and nothing good, I'll wager," Tam retorted. "Tell 'er what you know of that fisherman you had the muxta off of—if you know more'n I do."

The bloodshot eyes turned to him briefly. "And what d'you know?"

"Not much. Followed the bog lights, didn't he? And turned up witless?"

Instead of answering, Bruman fell to studying the bagpipes Saaski carried slung across her back. "Can ye play those proper?" he asked her.

"I can."

"Let's hear you."

No need to urge. Saaski swung the instrument into position and piped one of the tunes Tam had taught her, following it with an eerie one of her own. Bruman's good foot was tapping before she finished, and his whiskery face split in a grin. He said suddenly, "They'll have 'em off you."

Startled at his change of tone—it had turned faintly malicious, like his smile—she could only stare at him.

"The pipes!" he said. "*Them Ones*'ll have 'em, sure, if you don't take care. Steal 'em the minute your head's turned. Oh, they're tricky, they are. Tricked old Fergil, didn't they? Aye, he told me once. One of them Moorfolk-creeturs it was. Just tricked 'im blind."

"How'd they do it?" asked Saaski, wide-eyed.

Bruman was silent a long moment, his face unreadable and his thoughts perhaps straying elsewhere, for all she could tell. "He'd never say," he answered finally. "Might be a lie. I've heerd tell 'twas Fergil tricked the Fairy, and the creetur paid him out for it by makin' him queer in his head. No sayin' which is the truth of it." He paused again, scratched at his stubbled cheek, and abruptly dismissed the subject. "You, boy, fetch me out the ale jug from the hut. Then git back to your goats."

He bent his head to his boot mending—plainly the talking mood had passed. Tam shrugged and grinned at Saaski, fetched the ale jug, and they left, pulling up their hoods as a gentle rain began again.

Descending the slopes to Torskaal a short while later, Saaski mulled over the three tales she'd heard about the fisherman—none much like the others, except they all blamed some eldritch creature. She decided to ask Old Bess.

And Old Bess's tale, while different from the rest, and including more fact than fancy, yet had to do with an unearthly creature and some unknown happening on the moor.

"It must be fifteen years ago, child, when he first came to Torskaal. Maybe more. Late afternoon—half the village was coming and going in the street. And here came this stranger down out of the moor, all ragged and haggard, half-daft already, I don't doubt, and staring into one face after another, asking for his kin."

But those he asked after were long dead—grandparents and great-grandparents of the one middle-aged woman who remembered their names. And even she knew of no "Fergil" in her family except a lost great-uncle, a fisherman, who'd left the village five-and-fifty years before and never did come home. The family'd always assumed he was drowned in Moor Water, or maybe lost at sea.

Nay, not at sea, he'd said then, staring around in a way to give a body a fright. *Not in Moor Water. In the Mound, it was, where I was lost. She coaxed me into the Mound.*

Everybody had heard of humans beguiled by the Folk and enticed away into their secret home. Nobody had ever personally known such a human—or believed they saw one in this wild-eyed old man. Most crossed themselves, to be on the safe side, and hustled their children into the house.

"He soon gave up asking, poor fellow," Old Bess finished. "Went off to Moor Water and built his hut, started fishing,

116

and turned his back on the village, got more lone and odd the more years passed."

Saaski was silent, her skin deliciously crawling. A phrase echoed somewhere in the depths of her mind: *Time runs different in the Mound.* Someone had said that once—she could almost hear the voice. But it could have been anybody. She had heard numberless stories about the Folk and their tricks and their hidden homeland somewhere inside the hills. She did not ask Old Bess if she believed this one. It did not occur to her to ask herself. Strange things happened; everyone knew they did. And some were past explaining.

12

For Saaski, there were strangenesses even about the moor. Elusive shreds of half-remembered stories (or half-imagined dreams?) swirled unexpectedly around certain rocks and berry bushes, crept across the coarse grasses, or clung in hollows, very like the wisps of fog that forever came and went. She picked her mental way around them as automatically as she picked her way through a bog, wary of bringing one into clearer focus.

Occasionally one tricked her, as in the matter of the sheep wool. By mid-June shearing was nearly done, but there were still gleanings to be had on the high slopes where flocks, now nibbling other hillsides tidy, had grazed in winter. To Saaski, absently plucking tufts of wool off the brambles as she wandered homeward one day, gathering it seemed as familiar a chore as twig collecting. She brought

Anwara a good bundle of wool, along with a handful of spiderweb she had chanced upon.

But Anwara's reaction was disconcerting. "What's this, then? Why, you know I never bother with these tattered, stickery bits when we've got good fleeces. . . . Eh, well, it's all right, child," she added hastily after a glance at Saaski. "They'll do for scrubbing pads." Then, as she caught sight of the wad of cobweb Saaski held out, "Luddamercy, and what is that for, pray?"

For thread, for cloth, for strong thin cord, thought Saaski, but she jammed the wad back in her pocket and said quickly, "I brought it for the gran'mum—it stops bleeding and such." And that was so—Old Bess always kept a supply of web in a small wooden box on a shelf above her hearth. *For sure that's why I brought it*, Saaski told herself. Nobody spins cobweb.

Yet she knew the feel of fishline twisted of cobweb. And she could almost see the cloth—finer, stronger than any woven of wool or flax—silvery, shimmering, airy as the skin of a bubble. Surely she *had* seen it. Somewhere. Some time. And had gleaned wool, too.

The subject encountered a closed door in her mind. Old Bess was glad to get the web.

Old Bess welcomed all her haphazard offerings, but Saaski soon learned what to search for to add to the old woman's store of healing simples—buckbean, now in rosy, white-fringed bloom throughout the bogs, bearberry, and certain mosses. And in the highlands she gathered stonecrop with its fat leaves and yellow stars, which Old Bess liked for supper mixed with dandelion greens and a little oil and apple vinegar. Saaski, once she had tasted this odd dish, liked it, too. She did not mind being odd in the same ways Old Bess was.

She knew she was growing ever odder in the eyes of the village. "That Bretla, Jankin's sister, she sasses me bad as he does, and she's a whole year younger'n me," she told Tam indignantly one day as they dawdled along after the goats.

"What's she say, then?"

"That my toes're too long. And I've got devil's eyes. Says I'm not to look at her." Saaski spread out a hand and stared at it crossly. "Fingers, too," she added. "Let's see yours."

Tam showed her a sturdy sun-browned hand, fingers longish and supple if grubby and ragged nailed—but not as long as her fingers, it was easy enough to see.

"Don't heed what they say," he scoffed, thrusting his hand into his pocket. "They're ninnies, the most of 'em. That Robin, he's even too noddleheaded to know about the King's Town. Told me I'd made it up." He grinned at her sideways, showing the little gap, and she felt her lips curving in reluctant response, though she turned them down again at once.

"Well enough for *you* to say 'don't heed 'em,'" she pointed out. "I'm feared not to, lest they do me a mischief."

"What mischief, then?"

"Any they can! That Herewic—Cattila's big lad—he pushed me into the woods pond t'other day. Or would've, hadn't I skipped out of the way right lively. It's deep, that pond." She shivered, not quite able to seem casual. It had been a shock, a fright—and led to a scary discovery. Nobody had tried to save her, not one. They had stood and watched. She had saved herself.

"You can't swim?" Tam asked her.

"I dunno." She forced the quaver out of her voice. "Leastways, I never tried, and I didn't fancy learning that way! I'd'a drowned, I think."

"How'd you get out, then?"

"Never rightly went in. Just dipped my skirts, like. There was a branch hanging over . . ." Saaski let the rest trail into an evasive shrug.

It hadn't really been close enough to grab, that branch. She'd had to leap for it—fly, like. It had almost felt like flying. And her swift scramble into the higher branches had felt like running—effortless, sure, unhesitating, feet and hands working without conscious thought. Only when she sat perched in a safe crotch, heart pounding, peering down at the gaping, upturned faces of Robin and Bretla and Bran and Jankin and Morgan and Eluna and the rest, did she realize she'd just shown herself a good deal odder than before. She hadn't climbed a tree that way in years with anybody watching. She'd been careful not to.

Too late now to pretend she couldn't do it—that she was just like them. She wasn't. She couldn't understand the things they did. She wasn't like anybody she knew— even Tam.

"Don't heed 'em," Tam said again, but he was watching her face and he sounded angry. "Howsomever, don't turn your back on 'em, either! Stupid, murtherin' clodpoles. Here! Sit down—I'll show you a new trick I've been workin' at."

He pushed her gently to a seat and produced from his leathern pouch five smooth creek stones the size of

121

walnuts—a black one, a white, a brown, and two he had colored, one with red earth, and the other with a golden, transparent yellow he must have begged when somebody was washing a beehive to make mead. They were pretty, there in his cupped hands like some kind of strange bird's eggs, and Saaski could not help smiling.

"That's better!" Tam said. "Now watch—see if you can say which color'll come up next!"

He began to juggle—slowly, so she could follow the movements, tossing the stones in a lazy oval in the air, catching them again in reverse order. It was easy—she was soon naming their colors shrilly as they came thunking back into his hand. But then the lazy oval gradually speeded into a whirl, and once he seemed to have found three white stones somewhere in the air. By the time he caught them all in the pouch, and buckled its flap, Saaski was shrieking with delight.

Tam gave a pleased grin, swaggered a bit, and they thought no more—that day—of the village children. But it was hard for Saaski to forget them for long, for at the tasks they shared she could not avoid them—nor they, her. Until she could escape to the moor, the daily taunts and snubs and pinpricks of malice ever repeated *freaky-odd*.

Tam got angrier about it than she did. "Don't you hate 'em for treating you like that?" he demanded one day when she'd appeared with a skinned and bloody forearm—souvenir of a push she hadn't seen coming, which had thrust her painfully against the pasture's stone wall.

She was pressing a bit of web over the place, and only shrugged. She didn't really understand about hate. She often felt scowly, sometimes sore and lonely, mostly bored to screaming with their tireless, stupid pestering. But hate? "What's it feel like, hate?" she asked him after a moment. It was all right to ask Tam things like that; he never gaped at her for not knowing.

But this time he didn't seem to know how to answer. "Well . . . mean, like. You want to hurt somebody a-purpose, or plan out somethin' wicked that'll make 'em sorry. Can't rightly explain it, I guess." He hesitated, then his face cleared. "Here, I've got it. It's all the way t'other end of your feelings from love. Clean upside-down from love."

Saaski studied him a minute. Hate sounded a lot like the way *they* acted, not any way she felt. As for love—was it like wanting to do something for Anwara because of the bagpipes? Likely she didn't understand about love, either. It was just one of the ways she was different from everybody else.

Tam alone never made her feel it; didn't even seem to care. "What's the good being just like everybody else?" he'd say. "Here—y'know what Divil did last night?" and he'd be off on a tale of the black goat's ways that made them both forget hers.

But today he was inclined to brood, to take her bloodied arm more seriously than she did. "A body'd think their mums and da's would teach 'em better," he grumbled. "I s'pose they never pull these pranks where the grown-ups can see, though."

"Sometimes they do," Saaski admitted, thinking of the hair pulling Morgan and Eluna got up to, screaming with fake laughter and saying Saaski's hair was only a sheep's wool glued on her head. Ebba only watched sidewise with an odd, twitching little smile, till Saaski herself fought free of them, then she told her twins mildly not to tease, and Saaski—crossly—to mend her ways or Yanno would hear how she kicked and pinched. "I think the mums and da's don't mind," Saaski told Tam bluntly.

"Well, I mind," Tam growled, but there was nothing he could do about it, either.

The goats had found a patch of thornbush, and were happily stretching their necks and even standing on hind legs to reach the tenderest twigs. It seemed a good time to rest a bit, and look out over the wild, high world. Tam dropped down on a sun-warmed stone, leaned his stick against it, fished out his long reed pipe and began to play a mellow, fluttering little tune. Saaski sat down near him. She had not brought her bagpipes, having fled straight from the pasture and her collision with the wall. But she was content to listen and let the music mend the jagged edges of the morning.

In truth, the morning was half gone, as she saw by a squinting glance at the sun. She would be late with the firewood, with the churning, with the loads of bracken needed to underlie the stacks of new-cut hay and keep them dry and mouse free. Late with everything, and she was sure to get scoldings from Anwara and roarings from Yanno, who was always grouchy when he had to quit smithing to go haying—and no chance to slip away to Old Bess and the books. Saaski sighed, and felt the day settle heavily upon her. Go now, to her tasks—and the children—or stay, and be late and scolded?

It was no decision, really. She would stay.

"You a-hungered?" Tam asked, putting his flute away. "I've some cheese in me pouch—and yon's a moorberry bush. I'll pick us some in me cap."

Saaski sprang up to help; when the cap was full of berries she produced her own midday bite—two of Anwara's flat loaves—from her apron pocket, and swapped Tam one for a chunk of his tough yellow cheese. They returned to their stones and sat companionably eating, Tam telling one of his tales about the King's Town, which she never knew whether to believe or not. She was half listening, half watching one of the scampering small figures—or shadows or whatever they were—that she glimpsed occasionally on the flickering paths. This one was not following a path, but lurking just yonder behind the moorberry bush; she saw a flash of red among the leaves. Next instant a small red-capped figure darted swift as a lizard up onto the rock beside Tam. And there it sat, in plain sight, scarce an arm's length away.

Not quite in plain sight. It was like looking into clear water. The far edge of the rock and the clump of broom behind were both waveringly visible through its shape. But she could see the shape, too. And it was no shadow, no mere fancy.

It was a little man.

He was no taller than the miller's little Octo, who was only six—but he had a straggly beard, and grizzled pale hair showed through a hole in his scarlet cap. The longer she stared, the plainer she saw him, but he seemed not to know it. He was watching Tam—and whenever Tam set his cheese down on the rock to eat berries or break a chunk off his loaf, the little man's hand flashed out—long fingered and deft, it was—and snatched up the cheese and took a mouthful before setting it back. Soon Tam would reach for the cheese and set the loaf down instead. Then the little man would grab the loaf.

Tam was still telling his story, plainly unaware of how fast his lunch was vanishing. Saaski could not help smothering a giggle as she waited for him to notice.

At last he did, breaking off his tale as he blinked down at the mere scrap of cheese he was holding. "Here! Did I eat all that already? Where's the rest of my bread?"

"It's the little man," she told him, gasping with mingled laughter and bewilderment. "Why d'you let him nobble it?"

Tam looked quickly where she pointed, looked all around, then back at her, flushing a little. "D'ye take me for a fool, then? Nobody there."

The laughter died out of her. Defensive, half-frightened, she pointed again. "That little man—he took a bite—every time you put a thing down. Made a good meal, he did." She stared at the little man, who was still there, but staring wide-eyed at her, now. "Can't you see him? Right beside you!"

Tam looked hard at the spot and made a sudden swooping grab, but missed by a hand's length. The little man was gone in a flash, diving for the moorberry bush, stopping to peer back at Saaski with one astounded, terrified glare, then scuttling out of sight among the leaves. In a moment a meadowlark shot out of the bush and flew away over the moor.

"He's gone," Saaski said.

She had Tam's full attention. "I saw a bird fly."

She started to nod, then stopped in confusion. She'd had an idea the bird was the little man, but now she thought of it, that was nonsense. She hurried to look behind the bush—and came slowly back. "Don't see him now."

"I never saw *nobody*. Just that bird," Tam said.

She stared at him, half-indignant. "Well, he was right there! Eatin' your midday! Where's your bread'n cheese if you don't believe me?"

"Nay, I believe you," Tam said gently. "I reckon you saw 'im for true. Bread and cheese both gone, right enough, afore I got more'n half! . . . Aye, I'll lay it was funny to watch," he added good-naturedly, as Saaski struggled with a grin. "I only wish *I'd* seen 'im. Or could've caught 'im!"

"Caught him?" The idea wiped the grin away. "What would you of done to 'im?"

"Eh, nobbut looked him over. He'd've taken no harm from me, I don't grudge a bit of bread." He eyed Saaski speculatively. "I'll tell y' something. Could've been one of *Them Ones.*"

Them Ones. "Y'mean—Moorfolk?" Heart thudding, she searched his face, feeling torn between excitement and alarm. "You're makin' up tales now, just to plague me."

"I'm not! Other folks have spied such creeturs, I've heard 'em tell it."

"Likely heard that rattlehead Mikkel goin' on about his

pixie!" Saaski swallowed hard, trying to sort out her emotions. "If there's Moorfolk about here, bet they'd never let *him* see 'em. Or me, either," she added reluctantly.

"Why not?"

"Why should they? Never show theirselves a-tall, do they, less'n they want a favor done, or if a body's done 'em a good turn already? That's what I've always heard."

"You did the little man a good turn, keeping your mouth shut!" Tam laughed, and after a moment she laughed, too. "Here, then," he added curiously. "What'd he look like?"

She was beginning to believe Tam had truly seen nobody but the bird. "Looked freaky-odd," she admitted. But the phrase made her frown. "Eh, I dunno."

"Come on," coaxed Tam. "He was little? How little?"

"No taller'n my shoulder—seemed so, anywise. Dark complected—like a gypsy. But his beard and bits of hair near as light as flax tow."

"Brown eyes, then? Or blue?"

That flummoxed her. "Not blue." She was sure of that. "Or rightly brown, either," she added less certainly. "More . . . well . . . greeny-lavender." She met a startled gaze from Tam and said hastily, "I dunno. They changed, like."

Tam was silent, sitting still as a rock, looking at her with an expression she could not read. He seemed stunned, dead serious all at once, almost sad. *Thinks I'm gulling him*, she thought. *Taking him for a fool.*

Anxiously she explained. "Seemed to *me* they changed, anywise. Likely they didn't, though."

After a moment Tam smiled. It seemed an effort, but the

odd expression began to fade. "I reckon they could've changed colors—or anything else—if 'twas a Folk creetur."

"Eh, well, I didn't mark his eyes special. Only the gypsy skin and fair hair. Or maybe 'twas gray! You reckon it *was* a gypsy? An old one. Runty. A gypsy'd swipe your cheese, right enough!"

"Gypsies haven't come through Torskaal yet this year."

"Might've come today. And they're all thieving rascals, my da' says."

"Aye, maybe. But I never run across one I couldn't *see*."

Saaski made no comment. *She* had seen him. Seen his odd-colored eyes, the hole in his cap. Tam simply hadn't been looking. Or maybe it was like the runes, which she could see and Old Bess could not. There was no explaining some things. No sense trying.

But it was hard to believe that she'd caught a glimpse of one of the Moorfolk. Everybody knew you had to be special, someway, to do that. And if she was, she couldn't think how.

Abruptly she stood up, ending the subject. "I'm away to my tasks, now. I'm fearful late."

She was already on her swift way down the slope as Tam called after her—in his normal, cheerful voice, "Come back tomorrow! And bring your pipes!"

13

Just one week later, the gypsies came to Torskaal, arriving at midmorning—an excitement of decorated, hooded wagons and long-maned horses, dark-eyed men and women, and their tangle-haired, light-fingered children, all jingling with bells and hung with tattered bright ribbons and offering everything from tin mending and copper work to reading the future in a body's palm. For a few hours they were all over the village, bartering whatever they had for flour and honey and dried peas, hanks of wool and bladders of lard. Several went to Old Bess for herbs or simples, or with ailing little ones. The children, gypsy and villager, ran shrieking from one end of the street to the other, or taught one another dances and games. By midafternoon the wagons were leaving, winding up onto the moor beyond Old Bess's cottage on the track to the town some leagues away.

Saaski missed the whole entrancing spectacle. Or nearly the whole. However, she saw and heard a few odd things herself that morning—one of them stranger than gypsies, and a deal more unsettling.

The morning began with a bit of good luck that nevertheless threw this day out of kilter from milking time on.

The milking itself went well; she emptied her pail into the churn, then refilled it with water and lugged it into the long back garden while Anwara took the larger bucket to the well. They needed much water lately. It was retting time for the flax; Yanno had cut the crop some days before, and Anwara had combed out the linseeds for Old Bess to make into poultices and calf-brew. Now the stalks lay spread in a sun-warmed, water-filled stone trough beside the garden, soaking to loosen the hidden fibers from their woody bark.

Saaski replenished their bath, shook her wooden pail to get the last drops, then stood looking about at the morning and sniffing the rosemary-scented air. The rosemary grew at the farthest end of the garden near Yanno's bee skeps, for the bees loved it, too. As Saaski glanced that way, her attention sharpened. Just there by the big skep, a small, dark, vibrating cloud—growing larger every second—was hanging outside the slit door. As she watched, the cloud rose; a stream of bees streaked out of the hive and began to trace great circles in the air.

At last! Near a month after the other two, the bees in the big hive were swarming. Yanno must be told—and told quickly, so he could drop everything to get the new skep ready.

What luck! thought Saaski, as she sped back down the garden, still clinging to her pail, leaping over the carrot rows and little cabbages—what great luck, that she chanced to be there, to see which direction they flew. She could follow the swarm, mark where it settled, and keep watch till Yanno had exchanged the new skep for the old and scented it temptingly with herbs, and come to capture his bees again. They had worked together so, other years. It was a kind of game—hard-won but exciting.

"Da'! Da'!" she yelled, before he could possibly have heard her over the noise he was making at the anvil. A glance over her shoulder showed her the great circles drawing in, the stream of bees thickening into a mass. They would be off in another instant. "*Da'!*" she shrieked, plunging around the corner of the cottage, still scanning the air over the thatch. Yanno thrust an alarmed face out the smithy doorway just as she caught sight of the telltale little dark cloud, bobbing away through the sunny morning. Saaski pointed, still yelling, and was already on her way as Yanno cried, "Keep 'em in your eye! Drum on the pail! I'll find you, never fear!"

By then Saaski was cutting through Siward and Ebba's garden, sidestepping the cabbages by instinct, keeping her gaze still fast on the swarm. It flew erratically, soaring till it was no more than fist size, then dropping and recoiling and sideslipping in a slow, searching flight, but heading, all the same, for the wood. She was dodging thickets and stumbling over roots, the pail banging against her legs, by the time the wavering bee-cloud, beginning now to contract into a pulsing clot, dipped below the nearest treetop and disappeared.

The deep humming guided her to the spot where the

swarm had come to rest. It hung now from a branch, like a quivering oversized plum, to await the mysterious signal that would guide its flight to a new home. Yanno, who might have been a bee himself, so wise he was to their ways, had told her that scouts flew out, searched for a likely place, and brought word back—though he took care to get there first.

Meanwhile, Saaski knew what to do. No swarm would move off during rain or thunder—Yanno had taught her so. It was why she had brought the pail. She found a stick and began to beat her thunder-drum, scanning the nearby tree trunks for the fungus everyone called *pukka furze*.

She was still beating the pail a quarter hour later, when Yanno came crashing through the underbrush, bringing his saw and a wet cloth sack and the wood-handled iron scoop he used as smoker. For a while they were busy, Saaski setting the crumbled fungus alight in the scoop and waving the smoke back and forth under the massed bees to lull and pacify them while Yanno sawed off and trimmed a longish branch. When it was ready he flung the sack deftly over the swarm, pulled the drawstrings, and thrust his pole through the knot. Then he ran for home.

Saaski, staggering under the awkward burdens of pail, scoop, and saw, stumbled after him. By the time she joined him at the end of the garden he had freed his captives and stood watching. Smoke-drowsy bees were everywhere, bumbling into one another but never straying far from the big heavy-looking queen, who crouched sleepily on the landing shelf of the new skep while half a dozen regular-sized bees darted in and out of the slit-door. Making sure the place was done up to suit Her Pernickety Highness, Yanno grumbled.

As if *he* didn't know more about skep building than they about honey.

Soon enough they stayed inside, and the queen crawled through the slit-door after them. Instantly the whole swarm followed in a swift dark stream. In another minute not a bee could be seen.

"There now," gasped Saaski, letting her breath out and dropping her burdens with a clang.

"Safe and settled for another twelvemonth," Yanno said with satisfaction.

As they stood, sagging after their strenuous efforts, Anwara appeared around the corner of the house, shaded her eyes, then came hurrying, holding up her skirts. "So that's where you both made off to! Got them all, did you?"

"We did. And a good job we made of it, eh, Daughter?" Saaski nodded. They exchanged a glance of satisfaction. Yanno tossed the cut branch onto the woodpile. "All because the little one, here, came screechin' for me, and kept an eye on where they went."

Saaski, flexing her stiff fingers, swelled a bit at the praise. Yanno was smiling with none of the brooding perplexity that often shadowed his eyes when he looked at her.

"Well, I did wonder," remarked Anwara, "when I came from the well and saw the milk still there in the churn, and Moll still in the byre."

That brought Saaski down to earth; a glance at the sun confirmed it: she was late with everything.

But Yanno was feeling expansive. "Eh, now, wife, might it be you could churn the butter this one day? Take the cow, little one, and be off with you. You've earned a bit of play."

So that was the best luck of all, and Saaski lost no time getting Moll to her pasture and herself and her bagpipes to the moor.

Tam and the goats were not in sight; Saaski dropped down on a mossy rock near their favorite thornbushes, glad enough to rest her legs after the climb and soak up the warm June sunshine. The air smelled spicily of the marigolds studding the nearby bog. The tall spires of pink foxgloves leaned there, too, schooled by the winds to cant ever eastward, but propping each other up. Mixed with them were the purply red thistles that the goats preferred even to thorns. The fancy of goats for prickly things was a *right caution*, Saaski told herself. (It was what Anwara always said of tastes she did not understand.) But it made certain that this was a good place to wait for Tam.

After a bit she slid off her rock, swung her pipes around to the front of her, tucked the bag under her arm, puffed herself breathless to fill it, and began to pace—a few steps this way, a few steps that—and play to the summer air. First came a thistle-and-thorn tune, all full of quick, sharp notes, then a softer marigold melody, then a queer old, old song she knew about the sun, which always sounded eerielike even to her, and made her shiver. She cheered herself up with a thrumming, buzzing bee song, and that was enough piping for a while. She let the bag collapse with a dying yowl and stretched out on her mossy rock to get her breath.

The day was warm, windless, and still as peace itself, except for birdsong. She drifted effortlessly to sleep.

It was the bag, moving stealthily under her loosely flung arm, that woke her. Instinctively she clutched at it, blinked the world into focus, then sat upright, hugging bag and pipes as she gazed wide-eyed at what first seemed a dozen spindling little red-capped children gathered around her rock. But they were not children; wiry thin they were, with clever little faces older than her own. One of them had a long-fingered hand still on her precious bag, tugging slyly at it. She twisted it away from him.

"What're you about? Let be!" she cried.

They all went still as rooted things, their eyes wary, their odd little forms seeming to waver and go transparent like objects seen across an open flame, though she could still see them plain enough. There were only five of them, after all; one of them surely the same bearded mannikin who had nobbled Tam's lunch, the others younger, their pale hair floating from beneath their scarlet caps. It was hard to tell man from maid; they were all clad alike in an earthy, shifting green that blended like a lizard's skin with the moor around them.

One of the striplings still had a hand on her bagpipes. Again Saaski jerked them away.

"There! Didn't I tell you?" muttered the graybeard—not to her, but she heard him, right enough.

"Tell 'em what?" she demanded.

Five pairs of smoky-green eyes focused on her so intensely she could almost feel their beams. Belatedly, she realized he had spoken in some language she did not know. But it was plain what he *meant*, from the way he said it. He asked her something in the same strange tongue. This time it was gibberish. When she only shrugged, he repeated it in ordinary human speech. "I said—d'ye understand our talk?"

136

"No." She threw a quick warning scowl at the stripling, whose hand was again creeping toward the bag.

"You c'n see us, though," the graybeard commented. "That's what I told 'em. Saw *me* t'other day. And you c'n see us now."

"I can," she replied. Gathering her courage, she added, "Are you—Moorfolk?"

He ignored the question, instead demanding, "Which eye you see us out of?"

She knew better than to answer that; she'd heard tales of the Folk and their tricks. Whichever eye she told him, he'd strike that eye blind. And for certain she wasn't about to say "both." "Got eyes in the top of me head, like," she retorted, staring him down.

To her surprise he suddenly grinned, and his own eyes went bright lavender. All the eyes turned lavender; a ripple of laughter went around the group. They began to chatter in their other language, heads together, glancing at her from time to time; their expressions shifting from curious to wary to speculative, their eyes from lavender to green to dark. She caught words she thought she had heard before— they surfaced here and there unexpectedly, like trout in a stream, lost again in an instant. There was one that sounded a clear note in her mind, a little bell with so famil- iar a ring that it set her chasing through her memory, quite in vain.

The word was *moql*, and she found no meaning for it at all.

The bag stirred stealthily in her loosened grasp, and she snatched it to safety, the word flying out of her mind. "Let be, you sneak-fingers!" she snapped at the troublemaker, who merely grinned a little and kept his gaze on her face and his long fingers ready.

"How is't you know our tunes?" he asked her.

"They're my tunes. I make 'em up."

"Not the sun-song. Not the others, neither. Eh, I heard you pipin'. Know 'em all, you do. They're ours."

"Who says?" retorted Saaski.

"Tinkwa," he told her softly.

Again the little bell sounded in her mind—clear and somehow frightening, she had no idea why. "Be off with y' now!" she yelled at him, tears starting to her eyes. "All of you—leave me be!" Abruptly she scrambled down from the rock, hugging her bagpipes tight, scattering little people. She shrieked after them until all the five—last of all the troublemaking stripling—had darted away across the bog or flown skyward, looking for all the world like crows.

When she was sure they were gone, she sank down again on her boulder, breathing hard, struggling with confused feelings and longing for Tam to come.

Instead, she heard a rasping, ragged voice behind her, and whirled around to see Bruman the tinker raise his untidy head from behind an outcrop. "Told you, didn't I? They'll have 'em yet, those pipes o' yourn. They never give up."

"You saw 'em, too?" she gasped, astonished but in a way relieved. If Bruman could see them, for certain she'd not gone queer in the head.

"Saw 'em creep up on you when you was sleeping." With such difficulty that she wished she dared to help him,

Bruman struggled to his feet and stood a moment panting, braced between the outcrop and his crutch, the grooves in his cheeks deepening in a slightly mocking smile. "They was after them pipes, I knew they would be—oh, I've heerd about their tricks, I have. Then you woke up and *ping*, they was gone. But *you*—you kep' on talkin' like they was there." Slowly he hitched himself toward her. "*You* c'n see 'em, right enough. Here—which way'd they go?"

"I dunno," Saaski said. She backed away. "Ever' which way. I paid no mind."

"Must'a seen *somethin'*."

"Saw 'em scatter! What's it to you, anyways?" Again she edged away; this time he merely stood, swaying a bit, the smile fading. He seemed to have forgotten her. Doubtless he was as drunken as he could manage, but for certain it did not make him merry.

"Wisht I knew where they go," he said, as if to himself. He half turned to hobble away, then hesitated. "If y'see next time, come tell me, hear?"

"Likely won't be a next time," Saaski said with a shrug.

He gave a brief, sour chuckle. "Aye, that there will be, bantling!" Again he turned, settled his crutch more firmly under his arm, and this time did not glance back.

Saaski slung her pipes to her shoulder and ran in the opposite direction. At the top of the next rise she paused to look back. The tinker was making his slow, unsteady way toward the path that led down toward Moor Water.

Pity him she might, but she could not like him or his spying. However, she meant to keep the matter to herself, or

Yanno would be on again about a stubborn young one who *would* go onto the moor, come doom, come devil, however her elders warned her.

The morning, which had started so well, was going all awry. Giving a hitch to the bagpipes, Saaski plodded on upward, almost wishing she had stayed in the cottage to churn. Bruman's taunting chafed her. It was wounding to find out that the Folk, far from thinking her "special," only wanted her bagpipes—and dismaying to think they might keep at it, and at it, until she no longer dared come here. No better than the Torskaal young ones, they were—ragging her and claiming her tunes were "theirs" the way the children claimed firewood, and trying their plaguey tricks.

She found Tam just over the brow of the rise, stalking in her direction, hustling the goats ahead of him with a free use of his stick, and looking as cross as she felt. "*There* you are, then!" she greeted him, as if the morning were all his fault. "I've been waiting and waiting!"

"That's Bruman's doing, none of mine," he said shortly. "You seen him anywheres, by ill luck or worse chance?"

She saw now that he was more than cross, he was troubled. She nodded. "He's halfway to Moor Water by this time. What's he done?"

"Left the pony untied. Took me a three-league tramp to find 'er this morning, and she'd got her right fore stuck in a rabbit hole. Limpin' now. And last night I caught 'im kicking old Warrior out'n his way—kickin' 'im hard. I told 'im *one more time* you do that, jus' do it *one more time*—!" Tam was angrier than Saaski had ever seen him. Indeed, she had never seen him angry at all—only vexed, sometimes, at one

140

of the goats who wouldn't mind. Or at some other of Bruman's ways.

"What would you do to 'im?" she ventured.

"Leave 'im!" Tam's chin jutted. He gave a swing to his stick that beheaded several daisies. "Might've done it afore this, but for the animals. Never could figure what to do about *them*. Or him, either, now." He swung the stick again, but absently, and his scowl was easing. He gave her a flick of a smile. "If he's gone for the day, good riddance. Maybe he'll get too sozzled to find 'is way home. Where'd you see 'im?"

"Down by the thornbushes. He was—he was spyin' on me."

"Spyin'?" Tam's brows snapped together again. "What for?"

"'T'wasn't only me he was watching. Or only him I saw." Saaski chewed her lip a moment, hesitant to talk about her other encounter, she did not know why.

"This a riddle, then?" Tam inquired, with a tinge of left-over exasperation.

So Saaski told him about that, too—omitting her daft idea that she'd heard one or two of those Folkish words before; by now she couldn't call them to mind.

"The Folk're after your da's pipes!" Tam exclaimed, wide-eyed. "Bruman *said* they would be. Old slyboots! How'd he know? Here—you're not gonna tell me *he* saw 'em, too!"

"He did at first. Likely they didn't know he was there. He said I woke up and *ping* they was gone. They did go all waverylike," Saaski admitted. "Same as the one that nobbled your bread and cheese."

Tam nodded slowly. "You c'n see 'em anyhow. But him

and me can't—less'n they let us." He burst out, "'Twas my doing, that was—him spyin' on you. I went and told him about that little man. Now I'll lay he wants you to watch where they go."

"He does. I dunno why."

Tam heaved a sigh. Glancing toward the goats, who had found a moorberry bush thorny enough to suit them, he flung himself down on a grassy hillock. "Bruman's got some rattlehead notion about nickin' some of that fairy mead he's heard tell of. Barrels and barrels of it, stored somewheres, down where the Folk live. Makes you young again, sets you a-dancin'! So he says."

Saaski dropped down beside him, staring. "Gone noddy, has he?"

"No tellin'." Tam gazed off across the moor, his shoulders drooping. "You wouldn't credit it, but he used t'be a good enough fella. Good to *me*, he was—bit rough, but who cares for that? I learned to give 'im his own back, once I got some size on me. Fine leatherer—eh, wizardly! We'd go to all the fairs . . ." He broke off with a shrug. "Now look at 'im. I'd leave him tomorrow, but what'd become of the old gowk? Hurts 'im fierce to ride in that cart—and Lor', if we have to winter here, we'll freeze solid! Anyways—I like to keep movin', I do."

Saaski had almost forgotten her own troubles, listening to Tam's knottier ones, and trying to visualize the life he sometimes gave her glimpses of. "Where would y' go, if you left him? What would y' do?" she asked.

"Oh, then—*then*." Tam's eyes brightened and his grin spread like the sun coming out, showing the little gap between two teeth. "Then I'd go gypsyin' down to the King's Town, and all around to the fairs and the holy day doings, I would, and play me flutes and juggle and pass me cap and live like a lord without nobody to plague me but meself!"

Saaski listened entranced, seeing the world open out into a place of unimaginable variety, uncountable sights and sounds. "Could I come too?" she cried.

"Y'could!" Tam seized on the idea instantly. "We'd play our tunes together, you on your pipes and me on me flute! The city gulls'd be fillin' our hats with coppers, you see if they wouldn't! And when the snow flew we'd go on south'ards to the Long Sea, where it's warm all the year . . ."

He went on for some time, spinning the tale and inventing answers to Saaski's questions—each answer more fantastic than the last, until they were both laughing and Bruman seemed no more than a buzzing fly to brush off and be done with.

But soon enough Saaski came back to earth, looked about her at the familiar sweep of the high land, the ever-present clouds gathering on the horizon, and said, "Wouldn't we ever come back to the moor, then?"

Tam smiled and said, "Whenever we'd a fancy to. Come on, the goats are strayin'."

14

An hour or so later, Saaski wandered back down to the village, only to see the first gypsy wagons beginning to leave it.

She halted with a cry of anguished disappointment, then hurled herself down the last steep path beside the apple orchards, leaped goatlike onto the street, and fled along it to the cottage. She flung open the half door and shot in, stumbling over one of the hens and all but going head over heels in her effort not to damage her precious bagpipes.

"God's mercy, what has the child done now?" shrieked Anwara, reaching hastily to save her bread dough. "Is't a black boggart after you?"

"I've done nothing, not nothing!" Saaski protested breathlessly. "Fell over that addlepate chicken! It's the gypsies! They're leavin'!"

"Must, to reach the town afore nightfall. They've been

here all the morning. Thievin' us blind, no doubt," Anwara added, "so you best stay clear of 'em."

"But I never got me hand read!" wailed Saaski, stuffing the bagpipes into their trundle bed and giving it a kick back under her cot. "—and I had a lump of beeswax saved in m' pocket to barter for it! Never got to play the games . . . !" She was on her way out, headlong.

"Y'*will* go to that moor," Anwara said.

Without answering, Saaski raced toward the well, and the green around it that might have been a ragged-edged market square had the village been big enough to hold a market. It was to the market in the town that the gypsies were headed, but a few coppers more in their pockets always made a stop in Torskaal welcome.

The colorful turmoil of noise and activity filled the trampled open space around the well as water fills a bowl. Dust rose, harness jingled as the gypsy men backed their horses between the shafts of the gaily decorated wagons; the women stowed away unsold trinkets and yelled to their children, most of whom were still racketing up and down the street with the village young ones. A mixed dozen circled in a clapping ring dance; Saaski ran up to join it, but was pushed away at once by the miller's son Jankin, who cried, "Not you!" and his sister Bretla laughed, echoed "Not you!" and broke out of the ring to push her, too. Ebba's daughters joined the new game, as did several others; in an instant Saaski found herself in the middle of a jostling, shrieking mob whose laughter turned to jeering and whose mauling grew rougher, wilder, and more painful until her breath was knocked out of her and she felt as if she'd got tangled up in the mill wheel.

A large, thin hand reached in and pulled her out of the melee, held her tight against a comfortingly solid body in voluminous skirts, while a woman's voice berated her tormentors in an incomprehensible language. They backed away, scattered. The gypsy children who had formed part of the ring game—but not of the mob—stared a moment at Saaski, still gulping for her breath, then drifted toward the wagons. Her chest heaving, Saaski twisted to look up into the dark, stern face of a gypsy woman, who released her, steadied her a moment and straightened her clothing, then said, "Hurt? You?"

Saaski shook her head, though one cheekbone felt larger than the other, she had bit her tongue bloody, and both arms throbbed. She managed to gasp out her thanks.

The woman smiled faintly, nodded, and gave a final twitch to Saaski's apron. She was a tall, handsome woman, older than Anwara but not as old as Old Bess, with a scarlet kerchief half covering her smooth black hair. Saaski's gaze clung gratefully to her.

"Go play now?" said the woman, but she did not seem surprised when Saaski cast a darkling glance after her retreating tormentors and shook her head again, decisively. "Buy ribbon? Bangle?" the gypsy suggested, gesturing toward a nearby hooded wagon—though it was plain she did not expect to make a sale.

Saaski, however, grasped at a missed opportunity. "Will y' read my hand?" she ventured. She thrust out a palm to show what she meant, reaching with the other into her apron pocket to offer the lump of beeswax.

The woman laughed, nodded, took the beeswax, and led

146

Saaski to the wagon, where an old man and a young one were preparing to hitch up. There was a low stool beside the wagon's steps; Saaski guessed that the woman had been sitting there when the mobbing began.

She resumed her seat and took Saaski's hand, turning it palm up. "Goot fortun a'ready, eh? No hurt," she said teasingly, and bent her head over the spread palm.

At once her black eyebrows drew together. For a moment she went still as a rock, her grasp tightening until it felt to Saaski as if an eagle's claw held her. Was it to be a bad fortune, then?

Abruptly the gypsy released her. Slowly she raised her eyes to scan Saaski's face with a strange expression—grave, alert, a little pitying. With her left hand she made a curious gesture in the air between the two of them, then ducked her dark, proud head in what almost seemed a hint of a bow. Reaching into her pocket, she produced the lump of beeswax and held it out to Saaski, whose eyes swam with sudden tears—of disappointment, of simple hurt.

Pride drove the tears back and fought the quaver in her voice. "Will y' not do it, then?" she asked.

"Cannot," the gypsy told her.

"Is it not enough, the wax?" Saaski said on a sudden thought. She rummaged in her pocket again and found a silverweed root she had meant for Old Bess, who liked the red dye it made. "Will you have this, too?"

"Na, na, na, na, na, na, little one." The woman's strong, thin brown hands gently pushed away the offering. "I try read hand. Cannot." She met Saaski's baffled glance for a moment, then suddenly reached down and scratched a few

147

symbols in the dirt with one long finger. "You read," she told Saaski.

They looked like nothing Saaski had ever laid eyes on. Not like runes, not like the words she was learning from Old Bess. Was it gypsy talk? "But I don't speak your tongue," she objected.

The woman nodded gravely, once again taking Saaski's hand and this time pointing to the palm. "I don't speak," she said. She smiled, rose, picked up her stool and moved to the wagon steps, glancing toward the two men who were buckling the last of the harness over their team, then back at Saaski. "I wish for you—ver' good fortun." She hesitated, her smile fading. "But beware." Again she gave the slight, formal duck of her kerchiefed head, murmured, *"Dza devlesa,"* and disappeared into the wagon.

The younger man strode back, called something to her in their gypsy tongue, hoisted the wooden steps in after her, and slammed the door. A moment later the wagon was rattling after the others along the steep track that led past Old Bess's cottage and up over the moor toward the town.

Saaski stood watching the cloud of dust slowly settle, the first wagons appear at the crest of the rise as shapes against the sky. Then, with dread, she looked down at her spread palms.

They looked as they had always looked—smooth and pale brown, with a fine crease encircling each thumb and a wavery line, rippled like a tiny brook, crossing under the fingers. That was all there was to see.

Saaski swallowed, hid both hands under her apron. She had never looked closely at anybody else's palms. But there

148

must be something freaky-odd about hers. After a moment she headed up the street in the wake of the wagons. Their dust still tickled her nostrils when she knocked on Old Bess's door, and at the calm "Come in, Saaski"—Old Bess always knew her knock—lifted the latch.

The old woman was moving about her single room, putting away her little clay pots of unguents, resealing a cow's horn that held some tincture or other, gathering some dried roots into a wooden box. "I have been dosing the gypsies," she remarked. "They have cures a-plenty of their own, but they like to learn mine, too." She glanced at Saaski with her brief, one-sided smile, then her eyes sharpened. "And what ails *you?*"

"Nothing," Saaski said quickly. She pulled the silverweed root out of her pocket. "I brought you this."

"My thanks." Old Bess accepted the root, still eyeing her. "You have been on the moor, then? Missed all the hubbub and feery-fary? And you wanted your fortune read!"

"'Twas no matter." Saaski shied away from the subject, grasped at another one. "The bees swarmed right after milking—the last hive. Me and Da' caught 'em, though."

Old Bess was silent a moment, then sat down on her hearth stool and drew Saaski to her. "And how comes it your cheek is bruised and swelling? Was that a bee?"

For an instant Saaski thought of inventing some mishap. But nobody hoaxed Old Bess. "Tried to join the circle game. With the gypsy young 'uns and—t'others. But Jankin and Bretla—well, all of 'em . . ." She broke off. "A gypsy woman made 'em stop."

If Old Bess had nothing useful to say, she held her peace,

as now. She gazed at Saaski, and for a moment thought her own thoughts, which were unreadable in her face. Then she sighed, reached for one of the little pots, took out the rag stopper, and smeared a thin coating of some unguent over Saaski's cheek. It immediately felt cooler.

"It's well a'ready," Saaski told her.

Old Bess smiled briefly and said it would be soon. "I treated a dozen worse ones today, and bound up a broken arm. The gypsy young ones play rough, too—with one another," she remarked. "And never heed my advice. One little lad should have been in his cot, not larking about with our village imps. Burning with fever, he was. Have you other such bruises?"

Saaski shook her head, idly took one of Old Bess's hands, and managed a swift look at the palm. At first she was startled; it was a perfect network of fine creases—the deep one curving around the thumb like a richly branched vine, others slanting crosswise, up and down. There were many more lines than marked her own palm.

But her surprise quickly faded. There were also more lines in Old Bess's face than in most people's. The puzzle was still a puzzle—now the gypsy was not here to ask.

Disconsolately she wandered toward the shelf holding the books. "Will you tell me some new words?" she asked.

"I will. Bring a book and your piece of slate."

And so for an hour the uneasy subjects of bruises and palms were put aside, if not quite out of either mind, and the gypsy wagons trailed into memory.

Then Saaski went home.

It was not to be hoped that Anwara would fail to notice

the swollen bruises darkening her daughter's left cheek or, having noticed, would fail to speak her mind.

"There, now! Didn't I bid you stay clear of those gypsies! They play too rough for a little half farthing like you—no more heft to you than a sparrow!" Anwara sputtered on, turning Saaski this way and that, probing for other hurts, her hands as gentle as her scolding was harsh. "Where else did they hurt you?"

"Nowhere, Mumma!" Saaski squirmed away as the soreness awakened in her arms and shoulders in spite of Anwara's care. "'Twasn't the gypsies, anyway! 'Twas the others!"

Anwara's hands stilled. "What others?"

Belatedly, Saaski wished she had held her tongue. "I dunno," she mumbled. No use. Anwara soon had it out of her. Jankin, Bretla, Robin, Herewic, Annika, Alannah, Oran—also Morgan and Eluna, her own cousins. "They're always at me, Mumma. I don't heed 'em."

"*I'll* heed 'em," Anwara said, slowly straightening and staring first at her own tensely folded hands, then in the direction of Ebba's house. She did not seem really surprised—more as if something she dreaded had begun to happen. And whatever she did about it would only cause brangling or worse.

"'Twon't stop 'em, Mumma!" Saaski argued. "They'll just pay me out for it next time!"

"Is it so sure," Anwara said slowly, "there'll be a next time?"

"Nay, likely they'll forget it! If I stay out of their eye for a spell." Saaski reached for the egg basket and escaped before

151

Anwara could think of more questions. She hoped Yanno would not come to hear of it; least said, soonest mended. In truth, she'd brought it on her own head, trying to join their game. Should've known better, she told herself.

Whether Anwara told Yanno the straight of it Saaski never learned, but not to give Ebba a tongue-lashing was asking too much of her. She came home flushed with satisfaction, remarking that if Morgan and Eluna didn't hear of it on their backsides, she'd be astonished. No doubt they did; Ebba might turn a blind eye to their bullyragging, but not to their getting caught out. Naturally, the next time Saaski encountered the twins they pushed her into the mud outside the cow byre and pelted her with clods.

That seemed the end of it, to her relief. Her bruises faded. As inconspicuously as possible she drove Moll to the pasture each morning and escaped to the moor. Ten long June days passed in their accustomed way.

15

On the eleventh morning after the gypsies departed, Guin the miller's Jankin staggered home midway through the sheep-washing in the dammed-up brook, shivering and sneezing, with a head full of red-hot stones—so he told his mother, Berenda, and Berenda reported to the goodwives at the well. He took to his cot and by evening was burning with fever.

During the night his sister Bretla awoke with headache and shivering, unable to bear the morning sun in her eyes when it was time to gather wood. Nor could Cattila's boy Herewic, and by midday Guthwic and Faeran's Annika and her two younger brothers were ill as well.

Child after child succumbed. Within three days there was scarce a house but had at least one child abed, and at Guin the miller's there were eight, the two oldest having shared freely with all the rest.

To the goodwives, distractedly performing their young ones' tasks as well as their own, one suspicious fact soon became obvious: aside from a few babes in arms, the only child in Torskaal still well and active was the blacksmith's Saaski.

"Oh, I'm not surprised," declared Helsa, who being childless herself had leisure to gossip at all the village doors. "Have you heard tell, ever, of one of *Them Ones* fallin' ill? It'll be wonderful if that creetur warn't at the root of it somehow! You mind that bit of teasing the day the gypsies were hereabouts? 'Twas Jankin and Bretla begun it—and 'twas *them* two first taken sick! Clear as day she put a curse on 'em . . ."

"God's mercy, woman, can you do naught but caw like an old crow?" interrupted Old Bess, appearing suddenly from inside the house, where she had been dosing Gwyneth's Harilla. "If a curse it was, 'twas a gypsy boy's, and none of Saaski's. A lad I treated that day had a fever like all of these—and mixing with the rest however I warned him. I daresay half those gypsy young ones have been speckled as a fieldfare's egg for a se'ennight. Jankin'll come out in spots by morning—you'll see. Bretla next."

"*The pox?*" gasped Gwyneth, blanching and clutching at the door frame.

"The rosy pox only—not the bad one!" Old Bess told her, adding impatiently, "I dosed you for the same, when you were a little lass, can't you remember? It'll all be over afore Midsummer's Eve."

She brushed past and strode on down the street to see to Cattila's Herewic. But Helsa, enraged at the snub from one she dared not defy to her face, snapped, "Gypsy boy, indeed! Why, the gypsies were gone a fortnight afore Jankin sickened!"

Gwyneth stared at her a moment, then whispered, "That's true! So 'twas that—that changeling—payin' out all our young ones because a few played a bit rough."

"Should've been thrown on the fire to begin with!" Helsa whispered back. "It'll be the crops she'll put a blight on next. Or do the sheep a mischief."

"Oh, God forbid!" Fresh alarm drove every other consideration from Gwyneth's mind. "And our lambs so scant and late this year! Could she have done so already? Ach, what'll Edildan say!"

Helsa advised her to warn Edildan at once. Edildan, who had found one of his oxen gimpy that morning, passed on his own alarm to his near neighbor young Hungus. And Hungus, whose boy was still sick abed, had to leave off haying to fetch his new heifer from the pasture, lest she be "overlooked" by *that creetur*—and unjustly berated his wife for not thinking of it first. All the husbands were short-tempered and bone weary from eating cold food and having no help with the chores. In the long dusk that evening the liquid comfort dispensed at Sorcha the alewife's cottage only fanned the flames. By morning, when Jankin and Bretla broke out with spots just as Old Bess had predicted, the attention of the village men had already shifted from their offspring to their livelihoods, and their somewhat grumbling worry turned to deep-seated fear.

The fear focused overnight on the blacksmith's household, and the changeling harbored there to the endangerment of all.

The blacksmith's household had seen it coming. At the earliest rumor of curses Anwara, hurrying in from the well one morning, set the bucket down so carelessly that water splashed her skirts. She seized Saaski by the shoulders. "Tell me straight out, now, Daughter!" she said grimly. "Did you call down a curse on those young ones who savaged you? Even meaning no real harm—*did* you?"

"N-nay, I did *not*, then, Mumma!" Saaski stammered.

"Mind, I wouldn't blame you," Anwara muttered, releasing her and turning bitterly to hang her shawl on its nail.

"But how could I do so? I don't know how!"

Anwara studied her strangely, her expression a mixture of helplessness and pain. "They're all takin' to their beds, the young ones. Y'know that," she said. As Saaski nodded she added, "All but you."

"Well, I'm seldom ailin'! Nothing new about that."

Instead of answering, Anwara trod over to fill the kettle, her steps dragging. "Stay away from 'em," she said. "Stay out of sight."

Since she habitually tried to do so, Saaski held her peace. But a few days later, when Yanno came in for his midday meal and called her to him, telling her heavily he'd been hearing she'd "overlooked" Guin's Jankin and Ebba's twins, she was goaded into defending herself. "I've kept me eye on 'em, true enough! So would you if they did you a mischief whenever your back was turned!"

156

"Keepin' an eye on 'em's one thing. But overlookin's witchcraft," Yanno said.

"Well, what do I know of witchcraft?" Saaski was near to tears. "They're tellin' lies!"

There was not much new about that, either. But this was not the usual hubbub over trifles, and though Saaski took care to be more elusive than ever, it did not blow over. The pox itself ran its course; in house after house the rash appeared, then a day or two later the pathetic invalid turned back into an ordinary working child whose first complaint was silenced by worn-out parents. A se'nnight after the last rash vanished, the plague was a memory.

Then Helsa went out to the byre one morning to milk her husband's three fine cows and found one of them tangled in the chain ties, injured and dying, and in a twinkling Alun was no longer the richest man in Torskaal, but only a two-cow man like many another. The two-cow men and their families found it hard to be truly sorry about that, but all joined with Helsa in blaming the blacksmith's child.

Nobody could prove that Saaski had been out of her own cot that night. But nor could Yanno and Anwara, silently remembering her night wanderings, prove she had actually been *in* it—not all night long. They'd been fast asleep like ordinary Christians. So how could they know, Helsa asked anybody who would listen, what mischief that creetur might get up to in the dead of night?

It was a question with no answer, and it sent undercurrents of fear and ill will roiling through the village. One pale summer evening not long before Midsummer's Eve, a grim-faced little company of Yanno's neighbors appeared at his cottage door. They would not come in. Instead they asked that Yanno come into the dooryard for a private word.

Yanno put aside the new bee skep he was plaiting and stepped outside, but did not shut the door. Anwara, vigorously scrubbing out the iron pot with a handful of rushes, let her movements slow and go quiet. Saaski stopped sloshing out the mugs. They heard little but the rumble of voices until Edildan, whose high-pitched tones carried, remarked righteously, "It's for the good of the village. For the health of our young 'uns, and our beasts."

Yanno was silent.

"I'm told there's a good enough smith just over the moor in t'next village," remarked Guin the miller. "I might try 'im."

"Do, then, if y'care to walk a league," said Yanno evenly. "But the child's done no harm, and so I tell you."

"So you may tell us till doomsday!" said Alun. "We know what we know. She must go back where she come from— that's what we're sayin'."

"And where's that but here, then? Just turn her out, do I? A young one no taller'n my elbow? Man, you're daft!" Yanno snapped at him. "I'd never do it!"

Guin's voice came again, ominous this time. "Then if you won't, blacksmith, we'll have to deal with it ourselves."

"Ye'll deal with me first," said Yanno doggedly.

"We will if we must," Guin told him. "We'll give y'till Midsummer's. That's time enough."

Anwara and Saaski stood motionless until the footsteps

faded up the street and Yanno came slowly back into the house. He and Anwara exchanged a long, expressionless glance. Saaski waited anxiously, looking from one to the other, swallowing hard but not daring—not really wanting—to question outright.

In the end, no one spoke. After a moment all three went back to their tasks, avoiding one another's eyes.

PART IV

16

Midsummer, celebrated on Saint John's Day and the eve
before, had always been Saaski's least-favorite revel, one
she dreaded beforehand and avoided entirely if she could.
To begin with, the great Hillfire lighted at sundown,
Midsummer's Eve, on the highest point of the wasteland,
was always built of rowan wood, no other.

Saaski shrank from rowan as she did from St. John's wort.
Even in her first early days of wood fetching, she had balked
at having any truck with such fearful stuff.

"I'll fetch any other wood you like—but not that,
Mumma! Why does it have to be rowan?"

"It's a magical tree, that's why! A rowan fire breaks the
power of the witches, child—and all the other bogeys and
fairies and hobgoblins and who knows what all that goes
walkin' abroad Midsummer's Eve!"

"If *they* walk abroad, why don't *we* just stay safe in the cottage, and bar the door?"

"Because we light the Hillfire! Our grandda's and *their* grandda's all did it, and so will we! Now leave off your argufyin' and go to the thickets with the other young ones!"

But Saaski would not touch rowan. She would run off up to the moor instead, and Yanno would have to search her out and carry her, stubborn jawed and unrepentant, back to the cottage. There was no doing anything with her.

Every village family supplied fuel for the Midsummer fire; it was bad luck not to. So Anwara fetched the rowan each year—and endured the smiles exchanged by her neighbors not quite behind her back.

Besides rowan, St. John's wort was everywhere for the two whole days of Midsummer—garlands of it, woven in with yarrow and orpine and corn marigold, hanging on door lintels or around the necks of farm beasts. Not around Moll's neck—or she'd have stayed in the byre, unmilked, unless Anwara took over one more of Saaski's rightful tasks. But yellow flowers were everywhere else as June neared its end, and every year Saaski threaded her way through the dangers, longing for Midsummer to be done.

This year, the familiar dread was but part of the heavy, nameless foreboding of something hanging over her, which persisted even though the pox was well past and the children back to pestering her.

The children she ignored; she had endured their taunts and careless malice all her life. What was new and frightening was the grown-ups' grim attention, grown-ups' sidelong glances, grown-ups' voices dropping to mutterings as she passed. It was not mere young ones' mischief that was brewing; the village was uniting against her.

It had turned against Anwara and Yanno, too. Several householders had taken their smithing to the village over the moor. Yanno's anvil was sometimes silent all the morning, and he more silent still.

"They'll soon tire of a league's walk for a handful of nails," Anwara scoffed. "And the wives of their grumbling."

But she herself was being cold-shouldered by wives and men alike, wherever her tasks took her. Saaski had seen it—and seen Anwara's expression when she turned away, her head still high.

It's my doing, Saaski told herself, miserable but confused. She knew well what a blunderhead of a daughter she was— her spinning nubbly, her apron ties forever half torn off. She splashed the milk, she burned the bread. One look at Bretla or Annika showed how far short she fell of the daughter Anwara wanted. But Anwara kept an impassive front.

"She's not backward about scoldin' me for every little thing," Saaski told Tam, the day before Midsummer's Eve, as they wandered after the goats. "But when there's others around—savin' Da', a-course—she's on my side. Stands by me, she does. Acts like I was no different from the others."

She let me keep the bagpipes, too, and go to the moor, Saaski thought, feeling the familiar surge of guilty gratitude, mixed with the knowledge, more hopeless every day, that she *was* different from the others—freaky-odd—and there was nothing she could do about it. She could never even find a gift that pleased Anwara.

"Eh, then, why shouldn't she act so?" Tam said staunchly.

"'Cause they've all started takin' it out on her, that's why!" she retorted. "Turn up their noses, like, when she bids 'em good morning. And—they *say* things."

"What things?" Tam was scowling.

"Ask her how is it I'm feared of rowan—and yellow flowers and such. 'Oh, it's powerful odd, it is!'" she mimicked, "'Contrarious!' What's so contrarious," Saaski burst out, "about runnin' shy of poisons?"

Tam was silent a moment. "Most folks don't think of 'em as poisons," he said at last.

Saaski eyed his profile, then looked away, over the moor. "But bogeys and them *do*, you mean. Well, I know that, don't I? Why else is such stuff ever'where around at Midsummer?" It made her cross to think of it. "Seems to me bogeys just got good common sense," she snapped.

Anyway, that was all fool's talk, like Yanno's "overlooking," and half the street blaming her for the pox. She was no bogey; she was certain-sure of that. She glanced at Tam suspiciously. "Here—you won't be hangin' St. John's wort on the goats?"

Tam's still face relaxed into his sidewise grin as he glanced at her. "Nay, they'd likely eat it."

She tried to smile back, but it was an effort. After a moment of gathering her nerve, she said, "D'*you* think I'm a bogey? Or a witch or such?"

"Don't be a noddy! How could I think such a thing?"

"Well—what *do* you think?"

He was silent much longer, chewing his lip, his snub-

166

nosed, good-natured profile troubled. *It's something too bad to tell me*, she thought, as she had once before. But when he turned to face her, his blue eyes met hers squarely.

"I suspicion you might be Folk," he said.

For a moment she could only gape at him. It was so unexpected—so nonsensical—such a silly thing to say. And she'd never thought Tam silly. She hardly knew how to react without hurting his feelings. In the end she forced a bogus little laugh that embarrassed her. "Better than suspicionin' I'm a witch, I guess."

Tam flushed. "I'm not just raggin' you! I've wondered about it. Often. Mebbe I'm a lackwit. Leastwise I can see *you* think so."

"I don't!" Saaski touched his hand in brief apology. "It's only . . . seems a tomfool kind of notion."

"It's not, then! Don't they hang around you? Let you see 'em? Can't you see 'em whether they let you or not?"

For an arrested moment she considered this, but then remembered the runes, the paths. "Always been able to see—things. Ever'body can do somethin' special, can't they? You can juggle." She shrugged. "The Folk just want me pipes."

"But—" Abruptly, Tam changed his tack. "Your eyes change color, too. Warrant you didn't know that."

"So do yours," she retorted. Indeed, right now, as always when he was serious, their bright blue had darkened to indigo. She laughed at his astonished expression. "Warrant *you* never knew *that*."

His slow grin acknowledged it. She went on wryly, "If I

167

was anything to do with *Them*, catch me livin' in Torskaal! I'd live in that Mound, or whatever 'tis, wouldn't I? Eatin' honey all day long—no gossips to plague me . . ."

Tam made no answer. But after a moment he shrugged and gave up the argument. "So it was a tomfool notion. You asked me—so I just said it."

"I doubt it's what they're sayin' down to the village," Saaski told him. "Behind Mumma's back—Da's, too. They'll be sayin' whatever 'tis to their faces soon, I reckon. Then I'll know."

Tam's own expression turned grim as he studied her. "I know one thing a'ready," he said. "Y'oughta stay away from all them rattletongues. Keep outa sight—leastways till Midsummer's over. Come up here to the moor. Goats'n me'll look after you."

So he'd heard what the rattletongues were saying. Something too bad to tell her.

The goats had found a thistle patch. Tam took out his shepherd's pipe. "Come on—we need cheerin' up."

She swung the bagpipes around to the front of her, and they began to fill the air with tunes. But for once Tam's uncritical friendship, even the piping, failed to clear her mind of troubles, of growing fear. Plainly there was reason for fear; both Tam and Anwara had told her to keep out of sight.

Only wish I could, she thought. For a moment she longed for Tam's notion to be more than fancy. Ever so lucky, those Moorfolk. Kept out of sight whenever they chose.

That put her in mind of a tale she'd always heard about

168

Midsummer's Eve. Maybe it was true. Maybe, since the Folk let her see them, she could coax one to do a good turn.

She left Tam presently and headed downward, but she did not go home. As soon as he and the goats were hidden behind the crest of the moor, she turned across the slope and picked her way through the summer-dry bogs to the patch of thornbushes where Bruman had spied on her a fortnight or so ago. To make sure he would not spy today, she peered behind every bramble bush before settling herself on the same mossy rock she had chosen before.

Detaching the chanter, she piped a brief, meandering tune without filling the bag to bring in the strident chorus of the drones. The sound would carry, but not far; she wanted to reach only one pair of ears, which she suspected might be nearby. The tune finished, she lay back and closed her eyes.

Very soon she felt the bag move stealthily beneath her hand. In an instant she was upright, grabbing a thin wrist. She held it tight, peering into the narrow, startled face of one of *Them*. It was the one who had called himself Tinkwa—the one always after her pipes.

"Leave go," he said uneasily, trying to twist free.

"When a pig can fly," she retorted.

"Well, I won't nobble 'em this time, you've caught me out!"

"Nor next time, neither. I'll take care of me pipes, right enough. That's not what I'm after."

He quit struggling and said curiously, "What are you after?"

She started to answer, then on a sudden thought pulled

him closer and peered at the palm of his hand. It was pale brown and smooth—like hers. Indeed, smoother. There was not even a curved crease around the thumb. But the wavery, rippling-brook line crossing below the long fingers was strongly marked. That was the only line she had *not* seen among the many on Old Bess's palm. Could that mean anything? Likely nothing. *Should've looked at Tam's,* she thought.

The hand she held twisted suddenly free. Tinkwa eluded her grab, but lingered just out of reach, eyeing her with a bright green, curiosity-filled gaze. She peered back, speculating, puzzling.

"What *are* y'after?" he asked again.

She had to make an effort to remember.

"Oh. Aye. Fern seed," she told him. "I've heard tell it'll make y'go invisible, so nobody knows you're there."

His wide, mobile mouth turned up at one corner with amusement—and down at the other with mischief. "Fern seed, is it? Eh, well, if you was to go out on the moor and find a fern patch—stroke of midnight, mind, Midsummer's Eve—you could get some. If you're quick."

"Aye, and the Folk'd be quicker!" scoffed Saaski. "I know that well enough. But *you* could get me some."

He laughed outright, a thin, trilling sound that sounded like an odd birdcall. "And why would I want to do that?"

"'Cause I'll let you play me pipes."

He was suddenly attentive, his eyes narrowed to lavender slits. "D'you mean right now?" He was already reaching for the bag.

Saaski pulled it away. "I don't! D'you think I'm a witling? I mean after you bring the seed!"

He eyed her measuringly. "How long c'n I have 'em for?"

"Y'can't *have* 'em at all! You can play the chanter. *I'll* hold the bag."

He turned away scornfully. "That's no bargain."

"Well, you'd be off with 'em in a minute, and I'd never see 'em again!" As his grin admitted it, she leaned toward him, coaxing. "You could get me just a pinch of fern seed! 'Twon't take much."

"So why d'you want it, anywise?"

She hesitated, then told him. "I need to hide."

To her surprise, his narrow face abruptly looked uneasy. "Who from, this time?" he said.

As she stared at him, uncomprehending, a piercing whistle sounded from somewhere farther up the slope, followed by an angry, birdlike twittering. As Tinkwa's glance flashed toward it, Saaski grabbed his wrist again—not an instant too soon.

"Let go, he'll skin me alive!" he whispered, struggling.

"Who will?"

"Pittittiskin! Can't you hear 'im?"

The name streaked across her memory like a shooting star and vanished into the general dark.

"Leave me go!" begged her captive again.

"Will you bring the fern seed?" she demanded.

"Eh, there's no such thing, y'oughta know that! *We* don't use such—we just wink out! Y'never *could* do it," he added with an exasperated tug. He glanced at her face and grew

171

more temperish. "When you was one of us! Don't you remember nothin' at all?"

When you was one of us?

He was gone before she realized she had loosed him. It had ceased to matter. She'd forgotten what she'd wanted of him and no longer cared.

When you was one of us.

I think you might be Folk.

She sat oblivious of the day around her, scattered words picking away at the locks of memory.

Wink out.

Pittitiskin.

Y'never could do it.

Slowly the shadows of the thornbushes lengthened over the moor's woven grasses, then clouds gathered to blur their edges and the birds fell silent; yet she sat on, still as the rock she perched on, her mind reverberating with fragments of speech, echoes of voices.

Clumsy youngling!

Moql. Moql'nkkn.

What's your name, m'dear?

Moql'nkkn.

Oh, is it you, little duckling?

Time runs different . . .

She can't hide.

Hssst! Stop makin' a bother.

Help me!

Time runs different . . . in the Mound. In the Mound . . . in the Mound . . .

17

A cold patter of raindrops roused her. She stirred at last, focused on the fast-dimming moor around her, slid stiffly down from her rock, pulled her cloak to cover the pipes, and fumbled her hood up. For a moment she stood, feeling upside-down, inside-out, groping for where to go, what to do next.

The answer came without real thought. She headed down the slope, moving dazedly, then ever more urgently—giving a wide berth to the great pile of rowan wood, high as a cottage roof by now, looming ready for tomorrow's sundown on the wasteland's highest knoll. She crossed the hillside well above the village street, now all but running.

And all the time her mind was a tangle of half-heard voices, half-glimpsed figures, half-puzzling knowledge. The door that had been locked was creaking open, and memories came back in jolts and lumps and finally floods.

Schooling House.

I see your mama! That ugly one . . .

. . . a danger to the Band.

Do a shape change, or a color change, or go dim-like . . .

Aye, a bit of trouble—about this size.

She descended to the street at the far end, slipping hastily through the thicket of hawthorn that screened Old Bess's little hut. Without waiting to knock she pushed open the door and stumbled in. Then she stood, leaning breathless against it, unable to go farther or think what to say.

Old Bess was peering at her in alarm. "God's mercy, child! What is it?" She stood up, pushing her stool aside without looking at it. "Saaski?"

"Am I Folk, then?" Saaski blurted, in a voice that sounded weirdly unlike her own. "Did you know it?"

Slowly Old Bess's face cleared; the frown of alarm gave way to something like deep relief. For a moment she stood as if gathering herself. Then she went to Saaski, gently took her damp cloak, and drew her to the bench where they had often sat together over the books.

"I have always suspected it," she said.

"The—the runes?"

"That, and other things I noticed—very early. Perhaps before you can remember."

"I'm beginnin' to remember. I—I'm tryin' to, now. I never did, afore. Mebbe I tried *not* to. I think I was scared."

"Aye," said Old Bess. "And I suspect *I* scared you." She spoke almost to herself, and before Saaski could ask her what she meant, she said firmly, "Now tell me what has happened."

Saaski obeyed—or tried to. But she started tail end to, with Tinkwa's *Don't you remember*, then jumped back to Tam's tomfool notion, then she had to explain who Tam was, and about Tinkwa, and before that the little man . . .

And suddenly she knew who that little man was. He was old Nottoslom who used to take the younglings out on the moor some nights, when they guarded the red-horned cows.

"Saaski? Go on, child."

"Aye—well—this Tinkwa, he kept plaguin' me, always after Da's bagpipes, and I—lately I've been afeard . . . the neighbors and them . . ." She hesitated, lifting her eyes to Old Bess's, whose unsurprised nod told her she need not explain. "And Mumma told me to stay outa sight, and so did Tam, and I—I thought of the fern seed and I cotched Tinkwa and I looked at his hand, his palm, like the gypsy did mine, and it was—it was *like* mine, and—"

Tinkwa. Of course! *The bold ones, the braggarts, Tinkwa and Zmr and Els'nk—*

"And you began to remember," prompted Old Bess.

"I'm still at it," Saaski quavered. She pulled in a deep breath, feeling dizzy and unsettled, not sure whether to be frightened or elated, or what would happen next. There were so many puzzles . . . She burst out with the most baffling. "If I'm Folk, how's it come I live *here*, in Torskaal—and not in the . . . the Mound, or whatever 'tis?" *The Gathering. Rough crystals twinkling far overhead . . . greenish light. The earthen door of Schooling House.* "Did I—used to? I think I did."

"Do you so?" said Old Bess softly. She hesitated, took Saaski's hand, and held it in a firm, sustaining grasp. "Have the neighbors ever called you a changeling?"

Saaski blinked, drew her hand away. It was no kind of answer she'd expected. "Eh, haven't they then! Call me 'imp,' too, and 'flibberjib'—I've heard 'em, they *want* me to hear. Well, that's nothing—they call their own young 'uns that, if they've vexed enough."

"When they call *you* that—I think they mean it. I think it's true."

After a still moment Saaski whispered, "What's a changeling, then? I thought it was some block of wood, like, stuck in a baby's cot 'stead of the—" She broke off.

"Instead of the baby."

Saaski could do nothing but swallow—and it was hard to do that. A real live baby—stolen away forever? *Mumma and Da's real baby?*

Old Bess went on. "It's not always a block of wood or a straw mannikin. Sometimes—it's said—they leave one of their own in exchange."

In exchange.

Why, you'll be 'changed, m'dear.

Wintertime. Cold. Fright. Smoky room; a man who wore iron, smelled of iron. Faces coming and going. Being picked up and jounced, dizzily trying to get her breath between screams. Straw tick crackling underneath her instead of soft fresh leaves and fern.

You'll be startin' all over.

"Why ever would they do that?" Saaski whispered.

Old Bess shrugged. "Some think they covet the human

babies because they're comelier. Others say they're ridding the troop of their old and feeble—or the misbegotten."

Saaski gazed at her in silence, feeling herself sink down, down, deep into a despairing knowledge from which the fog was clearing.

Well! You're misbegotten. Father's that fisher lad . . .

A red jewel, on a chain, glowing like a drop of blood against a worn green weskit.

Aye, you're neither one thing nor yet quite t'other. Pity, but there 'tis . . .

Not me! It was Talabar.

Talabar.

Oh, is it you, little duckling?

But I don't want to! I won't! I'm scared . . .

Oh, aye, the fisherman! He was lovely. Pawel, his name was . . . or maybe Harel . . .

But I'm half Folk, too! What if I never work out 'mongst the humans?

Hsssst! It's settled.

"I told 'im! I *told* 'im I'd never work out 'mongst the humans!" Saaski cried out. "I said so, I did! He wouldn't listen! He just—"

"Who wouldn't listen?" said Old Bess.

Saaski broke off, gulped a breath. "Him," she said softly. "The Prince." After a moment, and a few hard swallows, she said, "I mind how it was, now. He told me. My da'—he was from Outside. But my mumma's Moorfolk. So I'm cotched in the middle. *Pity, but there 'tis,*" she quoted bitterly.

Old Bess sat still as her own clasped hands. "Aye, I've

heard the tales . . . a young bride stolen from her husband—
a lad beguiled by love. Never knew if they were true . . . Did
they say your father's name?"

Pawel . . . or maybe Harel . . . Had she ever sorted out his
name, that so-beautiful Talabar? "I dunno. Can't recollect.
Yet." Saaski's jaw clamped with sudden rage. "I mean to
keep tryin'. And chance I remember, I'll find 'im and pay
'im out, I will! It's his doin', all of it!"

"Surely hers also," Old Bess said.

Saaski looked at her a moment without really seeing her.
"Nay, not hers. She's Folk. She wouldn't . . . know better."
This produced a puzzled frown, but there was no sense get-
ting into love and hate and all that, it was too hard to
explain. Besides, there was a question she had to ask. "Does
Mumma know about me, then? Does Da'?"

"I tried to tell them, long ago. *They* wouldn't listen,
either. They didn't want to believe me. Your mumma—
couldn't bear to."

"Can't blame 'em, can you? Once they believed you,
they'd want their own baby back. And there *I'd* be." Saaski
stood up, hitched the bagpipes onto her shoulder, picked up
her cloak. "I best tell 'em now, though."

"Wait—stay a minute. Wait, child—"

"No use waitin', is there? I'll never work out! I suspicion
they'll believe it this time—less'n they know already."
Blindly Saaski turned toward the door, flung it open.

"Wait—shall I go with you?"

"Nay, nay, I best . . . go alone."

"It will be hard, hard, hard for Anwara," whispered Old
Bess, but she was speaking to herself.

18

Closing Old Bess's door behind her, Saaski noticed the familiar rune, still glimmering there. It was twice-familiar now; she could read it without guessing.

It was nearing dusk. The rain had stopped, but except for one long golden slit across the west, clouds still darkened the sky and draped like a wet purple blanket over the looming slopes of the moor. In the low-slanting light, the grassy patches along the meandering village street glowed vivid green.

She paused for a wary glance toward the smithy and home. The street was oddly deserted; nobody at the well, nobody gossiping in doorways, not a child in sight. Old Fiach's dog was stretching itself near the old man's usual bench, yawning, hobbling away. Must be the rain drove everybody inside, Saaski told herself. Relieved of the usual need to slip home unnoticed, she paid no further heed to the track her feet followed from long habit. Her thoughts were on the unknown paths ahead.

How to tell them? There seemed no way but just to blurt it out. Likely it would be no surprise—if they'd known—or feared—or tried to deny—all along. No guessing what they'd say or feel. Might be glad it was over. Anyway, the telling had to be done.

But what then? What then?

Can't stay here, she thought. Never did work out, never will. People taking their smithing away from Da' now, king-and-queening it over Mumma. Just get worse and worse.

Can't go back where I came from, wouldn't work out there either . . . *he* said. Likely they wouldn't have me.

Again sudden rage and misery swept over her. *Pawel—or maybe Harel . . .* Eh, if I could just recollect his name, she thought, that wicked jobbernowl, wouldn't I make him sorry . . .

. . . wager that fisherman's sorry now he ever took up with the Folk . . . five-and-fifty years older the minute he stepped Outside . . . Her anger sagged as she remembered. By now that Pawel or Harel or whoever was likely dead and gone. *Time runs different in the Mound.*

Aye, well. First the telling. Then what? Get out of Torskaal. Away from Mumma and Da', she thought. Rid 'em of me afore they're made to get rid of me themselves. Run away.

Run away where? Never been anyplace else—except the Mound.

Tam. Come up here to the moor. Goats and me'll look after you.

He would, too. And never let on he knew where she was hiding. But what about that Bruman? Likely blab any secret for a jug of muxta. Not Tam, then . . .

There was a hoarse shout, so close and fierce it all but stopped her heart. A handful of sand—or something stinging—hit her full in the face. Another peppered her neck, her arm. Abruptly she was surrounded by figures, swarming out of nowhere, yelling and rushing at her, shaking yellow flowers, waving iron spades and hayforks, poking her with them no matter how she dodged. The iron seared wherever it touched, and the caustic pollen set her choking and coughing. Another blast of sand—no, it was salt, they were throwing salt, she could tell because it stung like angry bees . . . A big cross made of rowan came at her, loomed—

Sobbing with fear, she shrank away, beating at the weapons, the poisons, the enemies, turned and leaped— almost flew—toward the nearest house wall and ran up it, her cloak sliding away, the bagpipes jouncing about on her back, to dive into the rough straw of the thatch. Shaking uncontrollably, turning hot then icy cold, stinging all over, she scrambled frantically higher until she could go no farther. There she clung, hugging the rough straw pinnacle, the blood beating like a drum in her ears. Below her, fists and hayforks gestured, voices shrieked and bellowed, the big cross swayed.

Blurred with her tears and her panic, the contorted faces swam below her. She peered down at them, shivering. Was this *hate*, which Tam had tried to make her understand?

She blinked hard to clear her vision. The scene finally

righted itself; she got her bearings. There, close by, was her own cottage roof, and Moll's byre. This was the smithy thatch she was huddled on. She'd nearly made it home— but they'd all been hiding, waiting. They'd treed her like an animal. Now what?

Quick, get harder to see, then slide down t'other side. Disappear, like. *Do a shape change, or a color change, or go dim-like. . . .*

She tried her desperate best. *Never could do it.* She squinted anxiously down at her arms, wrapped around the weathered dirty-gray straw of the pinnacle, and gulped with relief to find them going dirty-gray, too. A bit too greenish— she'd always found green easiest to achieve. But near enough to the thatch color. Her bare legs and feet, huddled up nearly under her, were fading to greenish gray, too. Now to shrink as small, as thin as possible, and sit still as a lump of earth, or a hank of that straw . . . but keep the eyes moving, to watch for tricks.

The howling din below her faded into a gasping silence, as if every throat had sucked in air at once. But they were still staring.

It's me dress—me apron, she thought, her frail hope of escape tumbling into nothing. No good, they could still see that white on rusty red, and she'd lost the cloak. Worse, they gaped up at her now as if she were some kind of hairy-scary thing, which made her shrink and hurt inside as well as out and feel shamed, without knowing what she had done that was shameful.

"Look at that. Look at the creetur," a hushed voice said.

"Godamercy," quavered another.

There was a small flurry of movement as a dozen hands came up to sign rapid crosses.

"Eh, there we are, then," whispered a third.

She could see *them* plain enough in the queer low-slanting light, make out the upturned faces with their wide, staring eyes and afrighted expressions, all just alike. The neighbors. The villagers. Ebba and Siward and the miller and the potter and the weaver and their wives, and Helsa and even old Fiach—a score or more—and in the doorway, penned in by them like captured prisoners, Yanno and Anwara, pale as specters, staring, too.

"D'ye believe me now?" came a shrill voice. Helsa was pointing a shaking finger. "D'ye see what I've been a-telling you all this time? Does it look like a child *now*, that cree-tur? Well, does it?"

There was a confused chorus of "ayes" and "nays," and a nervous shifting as those in the front burrowed into the middle, looking over their shoulders, and those in the middle backed up.

"It can't hex us once we're rid of it!" yelled Helsa, though she was backing up too.

"Aye, rid of it! . . . rid of it! . . . rid of it!" came the panicky echoes.

Suddenly Yanno's deep roar cut across the gabble.

"Enough!" he bellowed. His voice was shaking. "I've had enough, I have!" He took a rough step forward, pushing his way, towering over the lot of them and looking broad as his own house. "Begone from my dooryard, all of ye, with your

183

screechin' and your hayforks! Ye've proved what ye set out to prove, now clear off!"

Guin the miller stood his ground. "Ye know well that's not the end of it, blacksmith. There's sommat must be done!"

"Not by you and your nidderin', brayin' mob!"

"You'd have us leave it t'luck, would y'? Well, I say it's time to make our own luck! I say—"

"Ye'll leave it to me and mine!" Yanno roared.

There was a moment of silent struggle, the two men face-to-face. Then the rearmost edges of the crowd began to melt away; hands flickered across chests, shawls were pulled over heads, a few figures sidled up the darkening street.

Guin spoke again, his voice portentous as a rumbling of thunder. "See to it, then. Ye've got till tomorrow's sundown. *Then we'll be back*—to do what Christian men must do."

With a last expressionless glance toward Saaski, he headed up the street toward the mill. Silently the huddled villagers edged apart. In ones and twos, turning their eyes away from the rooftop only at the last minute, they went their ways. Only when the final faint thump of a closing door sounded through the dusk did Saaski draw a shuddering long breath, revert with a rush to her usual shape and color, and look down at Yanno and Anwara.

No need to tell them now.

They were still standing in the dooryard gazing up at her. Anwara's thin face looked carven, her cheekbones fragile, her expression one Saaski had no trouble recognizing. Anwara, too, was sinking down, down, into long-denied knowledge from which the fog had been mercilessly cleared.

Yanno—Yanno was *weeping*. He was looking straight at

her, his eyes glittering with tears and his broad, rough-hewn face twisting grotesquely. Abruptly he moved close under the fringe of thatch and held up his arms to her.

"Come down," he said in a strange, thick voice. "Slide down, little one. I'll catch you."

Saaski tried to obey. But it was hard to unclench her fingers from the pinnacle, painfully hard to unwrap her arms from it and make the rest of her body move. Slowly, stiffly, she hitched the bagpipes' strap up on her shoulder and eased feet-first down the slope of the roof into Yanno's waiting arms. He cradled her against him, bagpipes and all, and carried her into the house.

The room was thick with shadows, hovering and dancing away from the light of the hearth fire.

"Wife. A rushlight," he told Anwara.

She had followed them in to stand, still carven and wordless, just inside the door. Like a sleepwalker she moved to the cupboard, found a tallow-dipped rush and its holder, bent to the hearth, and straightened to set the flickering light on the table.

"Food, now," said Yanno.

Anwara turned back, swung the pot off the fire and reached for the bowls and wooden spoons.

Lowering Saaski to her stool beside the table, Yanno freed her from the bagpipes, and himself tucked them into the truckle bed, then sat down heavily beside her. She watched him, feeling muddled and weary, gingerly exploring the raw spots where the iron things had touched her and the salt had stung. His eyes were still wet; his jaw like a rock.

"I was on me way to tell you," she ventured. "Didn't

know, meself, till an hour ago. Never meant to hoax you. Never meant to—be 'changed. 'Twasn't my doing."

Yanno made as if to speak, but his lips trembled; he ended by nodding hard.

After a moment she gathered herself to ask what she must know. "Da'?" She swallowed painfully. "Da', what do they mean to do with me, tomorrow sundown?"

At the hearth, Anwara's hands stilled on the porridge dipper. Yanno tried twice, then blurted in a hoarse, rough voice, "God help us all, little one! That's Midsummer's Eve! They mean to throw you in t'Hillfire!"

It was somehow no surprise, though it made her skin crawl with shuddering. She stole a quick look at Anwara, found her clinging to the chimney shelf as if it were all that kept her standing.

"I'll never let 'em do it," Yanno told her. His voice shook but his eyes stared straight into hers. "Never. Never. Ye'll hide up under the thatch there, where you found me Da's bagpipes, and I'll be down here. They won't get past me, my hand on th' cross they won't. I won't let 'em take you."

Saaski gazed back at him, memorizing him, wanting never to forget. Was this *love*? Likely pity. But it eased the pain of *hate*.

"Nay, Da'. They'd throw a brand onto the thatch and burn me out. You, too. I know a better place to hide."

"Where, then? I'm feared they'll find you."

"Won't get a chance. They dassn't come out in the dark hours, you know that. Afore daybreak I'll be off. When they come for me, say I'm gone. It'll be the truth." Again

Saaski glanced at Anwara, who had started shakily for the table with a porridge bowl in each hand. "I promise not to come back," Saaski added softly.

Anwara set the bowls down with a clatter. "Ye'll go to that moor, that's where ye'll go, I know it!" she burst out. "Y'*would* do it, y'always would, I couldn't stop you, I couldn't—*keep* you. . . . "

"Now, wife," muttered Yanno as she broke off. "'Twasn't meant to be, that's all. Can't help what she was borned." His big hands knotted around each other. "Wicked. Wicked it is," he whispered, as if to himself. "Never harmed nobody, not a-purpose. So quick and handy with the bees. . . ."

Anwara, empty-eyed again, said nothing. She set bread and the buttermilk jug on the table, then winced as her gaze fixed on the raw spots on Saaski's arms. She turned and went out of the house, returning after a moment carrying Saaski's cloak and a handful of fresh plantain leaves, which she rubbed gently but thoroughly on all the places that hurt. The relief was immediate.

"Ehhhh, thankee, Mumma," breathed Saaski.

Anwara nodded, ran a hesitant hand over Saaski's tumbled hair, then tossed the plantain aside and dropped onto her stool. But she did not look at her food or at Saaski either, only into space—or into herself.

At that moment Saaski knew what gift Anwara wanted. And she saw the way—the risky but only way—to get it.

"Eat, little one," said Yanno.

Saaski ate because Yanno said to, then, after the first

mouthful, because she seemed to grow hungrier with every bite. Weariness eased and energy seeped back. She felt much stronger when she had eaten all she could hold, and drained her mug. It began to seem possible to get through the rest of the night.

19

She slept a few hours, came wide awake before moon-up and crept quietly from her cot as she had done so many nights in the past, struggled into her dress and apron, took her muddied cloak. Making her way to the hearth partly by the glow of banked embers, partly by feel, she groped for the bowl where Anwara always saved leftover bread for the hens, but it was empty. She touched her way across the shelf to the water bucket to get a drink, and encountered an unexpected sort of bundle. Her fingers soon identified her own lumpy shawl, knitted of the yarn she had been such a blunderhead at spinning. Inside it were two of yesterday's flat loaves and a chunk of hard cheese, the woolen stockings that she wore in winter under her clogs, and her wooden spoon that Yanno had whittled for her when she was first old enough to hold it.

She looked across the dark room to the corner where Anwara and Yanno lay in their cupboard bed. All was still and silent. Unnaturally so—not a single soft snore, no whispery crackling of the straw tick as Anwara, always restless, turned over. Not even the sound of breathing came from that corner. They were not sleeping, likely had not slept at all. But their wordless fare-th'-wells had been said.

Better so, she thought.

She put on the cloak, picked up her bundle, then felt her way back to her cot and pulled out the truckle bed. She stood a moment, biting her lip. It felt like thieving—and from Da', too. But it couldn't be helped. She disentangled the bagpipes from their coverlet, silently eased the strap over her shoulder, and as silently left the house.

Outdoors, she had always been able to see as well at night as by day. For an instant she hesitated, glancing down the dark street toward Old Bess's cottage, before turning bleakly away. There had been no fare-th'-well at all there, to comfort the parting. That couldn't be helped either. But she might—just might—see Old Bess once more.

A waning moon, thin edged, rose as she climbed the familiar path beside the apple orchard. By the time she reached the wasteland it was sailing clear of the moor's shoulder, outlining the dark, sinister shape of the great pile of rowan wood waiting there. Saaski hurried past with crawling skin, circling as far away from it as she could manage. A moment later she scrambled over the crumbling stone wall and was on the moor.

She felt safer there but walked on, steadily at first but

with ever-dwindling purpose. This was as far—almost—as she had planned. What came next?

She halted beside an outcropping at the top of a rise, and stood a moment scanning the half-cleared sky, the moon and stars winking in and out among the moving tatters of cloud, the dark moor with its darker shadows. By their look, and the feel of the chill, damp air, which smelled of rocks and heather, she judged it was still two hours and more till dawn. She dropped her bundle, eased the bagpipes onto a rock and sat down beside them.

Tam. No use waking him at this hour; last night's ugly tale would keep. Should she tell him what she meant to do? Or do it first and tell him afterwards—if there was an afterwards? Could she do it at all? She knew only that she meant to try.

But how to find out more of what she might need urgently to know? Her memories were scraps and fragments. Tinkwa would likely tell her more fancy than fact; he'd think it a good prank to hoax her. There was no one else to ask.

Aye, there was one other, she thought bitterly. Or might have been, once, that Pawel, or maybe Harel . . .

He was lovely—so handsome!

Ah. And he was among us here for quite a space, was he not, m'dear?

He was, Prince . . .

As always, the light, silvery voice in her memory broke off, just there.

Pawel, or maybe Harel . . . Suddenly, unexpectedly, the voice went on. *Fergil! That was his name, I think. Yes, Fergil . . .*

Saaski sat motionless on her rock, staring into the night. *Five-and-fifty years older, once he stepped Outside . . .* But *not* dead and gone at all. Fergil, the strange old fisherman, the old lackbrain, the old noddikins. *In the Mound, it was. She coaxed me into the Mound.* All his meandering, rattlehead talk was true.

Now that she had his image in her mind—the lonely, stooped figure, the stubbly face and mistrustful eyes, the nervous caution—Saaski no longer cared to pay him out, or make him any sorrier than he already was.

But she didn't mind making him help.

She slid off the rock, gathered bagpipes and bundle, and headed downhill toward Moor Water and the dunes.

He was there; his dog—a whitish shape touched with the glimmering moonlight—lay stretched across his doorstep. Saaski made no sound treading the sandy path toward the hut, but the dog woke, scrambled to its feet with nose and ears extended, found her at once, and barked.

"Eh, then, get on with it—tell 'im I'm here," she told the dog, and stood waiting, halfway along the path, in plain sight. When the door creaked, and Fergil's hulking, rumple-haired figure appeared in the opening, she said loudly. "It's me and I need us to talk. Make your dog leave me be."

For an instant he went rigid. Then, as Saaski told herself, it was a fair wonder how fast he could move. He was inside, with the door closing, before she could draw breath.

"Wait! I'm no bogey! Y'*know* that!"

The door halted, leaving a crack. Through it, Fergil's rusty, quavering voice said, "Go away. I want nothin' to do with the likes of you."

"A mite too late for that! Best to hear me out."

The crack was narrowing. "Nay, I'll not! Why should I?"

"'Cause you're my da'!" shrieked Saaski.

Alarmed, the dog began to bark again. But the crack stayed motionless, then at last slowly widened enough to show a glimpse of Fergil's shadowy hulk. The dog glanced up at him, whined, gave another indecisive bark or two, and fell silent.

Saaski said, "Wager you suspicioned it yourself—the day you heard me pipin' those tunes—and got a look at me. Well, now I *know* it. It's your doin' I'm here at all. And I need help, so let me in."

The shadow in the doorway seemed to droop even more. Then the door slowly swung wide. Fergil stepped out, mumbled something to his dog, and watched her walk past him into the room.

It was half the size of Yanno and Anwara's, twice as untidy. So much she could see at once by the low flickering of the hearth fire. When he kindled a stub of candle, the details jumped at her: a frayed bed made of coiled straw-rope with his old cloak tumbled on it; a crusted pot and wooden trencher; water bucket on a sagging bench, a stool, a mug, a row of capped clay jugs—likely muxta—against one wall, a tangle of nets and fish traps along another; a strong smell of fish, wet dog, unwashed old man, and melting mutton tallow.

Brawny lad . . . hair like a horse's mane . . .

He was lovely! So handsome!

She turned to face him and found him studying her, his eyes dark and moody but unalarmed. "Y'look like 'er," he muttered. "Not so comely as her—nay, not by half. But y'look like Folk. She, now, she was a rare beauty." His face softened, then went hard again. "Tricked me, she did. Gulled me proper."

"Shoulda known better than to follow 'er off," Saaski retorted.

His eyes opened wide and defensively. "Told me she'd come out'n the Mound and live with me here!" He added, with a kind of mumbling apology in his rusty voice, "I'd'a looked after you, I would, true, hadn't she tricked me."

What a noddikins, Saaski thought. Believe anything, he would. "Eh, well, it's over and done now. Past mendin'." She hesitated, then came out with it. "You could get a bit of your own back, though, should you want to. Pay 'er out proper."

He backed off instantly, all the old suspicion back in his face, his hands flying up to ward her off. "Nay! I want no truck with 'er now. You, either. Too late. Past mendin'. You said it yourself."

"Y' needn't have any truck with 'er. Needn't leave this room." She waited till his hands came down, twisted each other anxiously, finally dropped to his sides.

"How, then?" he asked her.

"Just tell me some things I can't recollect. About the Mound." She hesitated, swallowed hard, but held his gaze with her own. "I mean to go down there. Soon's I can."

194

"They'll never let y' stay," he whispered.

"Don't mean to stay. Mean to get a bit of *my* own back. They tricked me, too. Anywise, they tricked my mumma— my . . ." She didn't know what to call them, now. "Anwara. And Yanno. Stole their real baby away, that's what the Folk did."

"Aye," he said slowly. "I allus reckoned that's what happened. But what can y'do about it now, little 'un?"

"Steal 'er back."

Another silence, accompanied by one of his wild-eyed, suspicious stares. "How?" he said at last.

"Dunno yet! First thing is to find the way in. I used to know well enough where 'twas," she added crossly. "Do you? You found it once."

"Nay! Found *her*. I was just walkin' overmoor— Midsummer's Eve, 'twas. And I come across 'em sudden- like—a whole passel of *Them Ones* a'dancin' to a piper, and *her* amongst 'em. She come over and took me hand, and I danced with 'em, too. Wasn't so gawky and stiff then—only twenty year old, young and strong . . ."

His voice had turned mournful and dreamy, his eyes vacant. Saaski lost no time in rousing him from his maunderings. "So after the dancin'—where'd she take you?"

"Don't rightly know," Fergil said—as she'd half expected. Blinking, shaking his shaggy head as if he had long puzzled over this himself, he went on wonderingly. "One minute we was there, on t'moor, next minute, in a glitterin' big place, with a feast like you never saw laid out—all pheasants and peacocks and oranges and sugarplums on great gold trenchers, and goblets foamin' with fairy mead. . . . They

195

told me I dassn't eat or sup—eh, I paid 'em no mind . . ."

Impatient, Saaski quit listening. The only foods she remembered were wild herbs and birds' eggs—along with lentils nobbled from Torskaal storerooms, occasional rabbits from Torskaal traps. Certainly she had not dined on peacocks, much less oranges, which the gypsies talked about but nobody else had ever seen. That was all *glamourie* conjured up to hoax the likes of Fergil—first cousin to the gold-piece trick, that was.

"Never mind the feastin'," she interrupted. "What else did y' see? Where's the Nursery? Spinning House? The byres for the red-horns? Likely they'll be schoolin' that child in some such place."

Fergil merely turned wide eyes to her, and shook his head.

"Eh, botheration! You're no use to me a-tall!" she exclaimed. "What *do* you recollect? You stayed a right good while."

"I didn't! Leastwise . . . seemed only a little time. Though I were no lad when I come out," he added bitterly. "All 'cause I ate Folk food, and supped Folk mead." He swung around to her. "Don't you take a bite nor a sup, long as you're there, or it'll go hard with ye."

"Folk food won't hurt me—ate it in me cradle." She brooded a moment, watching the stub of candle flickering, giving out more smell than light, a drop of tallow rolling over its lip. "So y' came out. Where?" she asked him.

The spark of animation in his face died. "T'moor. Woke up—cold and stiff in me joints. All by meself. And old." He turned away, shrugging, bitterness in every line of his sagging shoulders. "Dunno just where. I mind there was thorn trees—tore me cloak tryin' to find me way in the dark."

Thorn trees. I might've guessed, Saaski thought.

Now it was she who let the silence stretch out, while she made a wrenching peace with what she had known all along must happen. She was roused by Fergil's dog, whining questioningly at the door and adding a loud scrabble of toe-nails for emphasis.

"Quiet, now!" Fergil growled at it, and the noise subsided.

Saaski sighed. "I'll have to find the place on me own. You're not much good to me." She looked him over once more, thinking of Yanno. "Not much of a da', either, I'm bound to say."

He took the judgment humbly, twisting his knobby hands together and nodding. "Help you if'n I could, little 'un," he muttered.

"Well, y'can. You will, too, hear me?"

He eyed her uneasily, but bobbed his head. She hesitated a last moment, then set her jaw and eased the bagpipes off of her shoulder. As she detached the chanter, she scanned the little room for a safe spot, a clean spot. There was none. Untying her shawl-covered bundle, she took out her spare petticoat, wrapped it around the bag and drones, and set them carefully in a corner. The chanter she tucked into her bundle. "Now, hark to what I tell you," she commanded. Her voice shook a little, but she fixed her father with a steady gaze. "Here's what's gonna happen."

A few minutes later she left the hut, watched but not hindered by the dog, who stood, like Fergil, shivering in the predawn chill until she was past the byre and out of their sight. She climbed over the dunes and around the edge of the woods, crossed the oak-dotted pasture above that, and found the remote clearing in the hazel thickets where the spring bubbled into the pond. No village children here now, to push her in. The place was lonely and safe, ringed in shadow; a few stars glinted in the water.

She dropped her bundle, and herself on a mossy patch of bank beside it, took out the chanter, and very softly began to play. She played every wild tune she knew, and every eerie, secret one, and a few quavering, questioning, keening ones she had never known until now. She played until the dawn brightened almost into daylight. Then with a last, lingering note, she let the first birdsong take over the music making.

Curling upon the moss, she slept an hour, the chanter clasped tight and safe against her. When she woke, the dew was vanishing in the morning sun. Slowly she tucked the chanter back into her bundle, left the clearing, and started for the moor, to find Tam, tell him the story of the night, and say good-bye.

20

She was climbing the shoulder of the hill that sheltered the tinker's reed hut and hooded cart when the goats appeared against the sky as on the day when she first saw them. Behind them was Tam, who stopped dead at sight of her, then rushed down the slope in reckless leaps.

"You're here! Eh, thank the good Lord! I was on me way to the smithy, goats and all—"

She broke in, with a wary glance toward the brow of the hill behind him. "Where's Bruman?"

"Dead to the world, yonder in the hut." Tam gave a jerk of his head in that direction. "Sleepin' off the muxta he dragged back from Torskaal yestereve—spent half the night swillin' and tellin' me tales . . ." Tam eyed her sidewise, his offhand tone at odds with his worried frown. "No truth in 'em, I dessay."

"Truth enough." She had not noticed Bruman's face last night among those staring up as she clung to the roof-thatch pinnacle. But he might have heard talk of it at Sorcha the alewife's—talk doubtless blown out of all likeness to fact by then, with witches and boggarts swarming thick as bees. "I'd best tell you the straight of it," she said. "That noddy idea of yours—'twas near on the mark after all. I . . . I been rememberin'."

Tam's face tightened, but not with surprise. He dropped down on the grass, prepared to listen. Sitting beside him, with the goats idling and nibbling below, Saaski told the tale of yesterday. Tam's gaze never left her face, the tension in his own gradually hardening into a sort of stubborn calm.

As she fell silent he took a deep breath, muttered, "Eh, I knew it, I knew!" Abruptly, he said, "You did right. To run away. Good riddance to the lot of 'em, *I* say."

"Good riddance to me, you mean."

"Here, you needn't fret, I'll look after you. Nay, I will! We'll go clean away, you'n me, to the King's Town, like we planned it once, play our music and juggle at the fairs—"

She let him go on for a minute, to cheer himself—it was a brave effort to cheer *her*, that she knew. But when he paused for breath she said gently, "Won't work, Tam. Who'd look after the goats, and the pony, and old Warrior? And Bruman?"

"Eh, *he* can look after hisself," Tam muttered, but he was scowling at the thready mosses between his feet, plainly facing facts along with her. The cart was Bruman's, like all the rest. Without it, the two of them would be heading for the King's Town on foot, and penniless, leaving the animals to Bruman's uncertain care. If they turned thief, they left Bruman to the northern winter and his pain.

"Anyway . . ." added Saaski. She took a long breath and told Tam the rest of her night's doings.

Only once did he break in, to exclaim, "Fergil! Now who'd ever've thought it!" but when he heard her plan to steal back the child, his mouth dropped open. "Don't be daft! Y'need to get clean away! Them villagers find out ye're still on the moor, they'll be after ye!"

"Mebbe not today. They're afeard of the moor on Midsummer's Eve." She set her jaw. "Anywise, I mean to get Mumma's child."

He was silent, elbows on knees, staring out over the moor. Then he said abruptly, "Well, if ye're set on it, I'm goin' along o' you. Into that Mound."

"Nay, you can't!" She turned to him in alarm. "Weren't you listenin'? What happens to me won't matter—likely nothin'. But you—y'might never get out! Or it might be . . . five-and-fifty years'd gone by and you'd wake up cold and stiff—and old." She could hear Fergil's bitter voice in her ears, and shivered to think of such happening to Tam.

"I'll take me chances," he said, unmoved.

"Well, you won't," she retorted. "I don't need a great gowk of a boy to look after, as well as meself! Be plenty to think of just findin' that child, I dessay—dunno where they'll've put her, that's what's plaguin' me. Or how to sneak 'er out without the Prince seein'."

"Or whether she'll come quiet," said Tam.

Saaski looked at him in dismay. Trouble from the child itself had never occurred to her.

201

"Will she be as big as you? Or a baby still?" Tam asked. "Or somers in between, like?"

"I dunno," Saaski admitted, beginning to feel a hollow sensation inside her.

"Ye'll need me to carry 'er, I reckon," Tam said in a matter-of-fact tone. "Or drag 'er. Or give that Prince a thump or two on the noggin if he tries to stop us."

"Eh, stop it! You're talkin' flapdiddle!" Saaski scarcely knew whether to laugh or cry. "Touch the Prince and he'd likely turn you to a hoptoad! Or somethin' worse. You'll not go in the Mound. I dassn't let you!"

"Mound, is it?" A new voice, hoarse and ragged, spoke behind them. They whirled to see Bruman swaying unsteadily on the lip of the rise, red eyed. "You goin' in the Mound, bantling? Say, I'll come along—get me a taste o' that fairy mead!"

"Here! Be off with ye!" Tam exclaimed, leaping up and starting for him, with a glance at Saaski of mingled embarrassment and dismay.

Bruman gave a laugh that turned to a gasp of pain as he staggered backward onto his bad leg. He would have gone sprawling if Tam hadn't caught him. "Have a care! Where's your crutch?" the boy muttered, easing him down on a hummock and after a brief search recovering the crutch a few yards away. "Gone witless, have ye? Let *you* in there and you'd never get out!"

"Eh, what'd I be missin'?" Bruman mumbled absently. His laughter had vanished, and he sat with drawn face, gingerly straightening the bad leg.

Tam stood frowning down at him, put the crutch where

he could reach it. "You're not to go blabbin' down to Torskaal about seein' us," he said sharply. "Seein' *her*." He jerked his head toward Saaski. "Not to *nobody*. You hear?"

"You mind your tongue," Bruman rasped, without glancing at him. His gaze was on Saaski, his expression now faraway and weary. "I mean y' no ill, bantling. Go your way," he said. Bracing his crutch, he heaved himself around to prop his shoulders against an outcrop, leaned back, and closed his eyes.

Saaski looked at Tam, who beckoned her with a jerk of his head. They moved quietly away, driving the goats on before them. Tam glanced back once, frowning, but said only, "He'll bide there till his leg's eased over the worst of it, then he'll go on to the hut."

Saaski wished she could be sure of that—and sure he would stay there. Wished he hadn't turned up at all. But it was no good fretting. "Likely catch his death if it rains much," she commented with an eye on one of the cloud banks gathering as usual in the west.

"No more'n those goats would." Tam's tone was absent, but his snub-nosed profile had a bleak expression, and after a moment he said, "Leg's gettin' worse, I think. Dunno how he's gonna fare when we have to head south."

South to the King's Town, Saaski thought, trying in vain to envision such a place—or any place different from this one she knew.

Tam spoke again, briskly. "Leastways he won't be goin' down any Mound. But *I'm* goin'. You'd best make peace with it."

It was no use arguing. Saaski merely said to herself, *we'll see!* In truth she did not know what it was they would see, or how she could stop Tam doing as he chose. But she dreaded what might happen to him. Her memories of the Mound were dim and muddled, strain as she would to call them up sharp and clear. She knew the Gathering would be full of goings and comings; it always was. A couple of strangers would cause no stir. Easy enough, especially on Midsummer's, for a human or two to stray in, beguiled by Folk or their own mischance. Getting out safe was a different matter. That took help—Folk help. She did not think being half Folk would be enough.

Tam's thoughts must have been something like hers. "Where *is* that door?" he asked her suddenly. "Can you get us in? And once we're in there, how . . ." His voice trailed off.

Saaski mustered a confident tone. "Never you mind. Got a plan, I have." She set her jaw, loss and misery suddenly wailing like drones inside her, and all but snapped at Tam when he asked more questions. "I'm gonna call one o' Them. You're to hide somewhere and stay outa sight! You mind me? No matter what you hear."

Tam halted and faced her, belligerent with worry. "What will I hear, then?"

"Nothin' but me, drivin' a bargain," she said with a sigh.

So when they reached the hollow with the thorn trees, Tam hid while Saaski took the chanter out of her bundle and began to play. The sound had never failed yet to bring Tinkwa around pestering.

Today he was tardy. She'd all but given him up when he was suddenly there beside her, laughing, snatching at the chanter. She wrested it away from him, caught his wrist. "Here! Hold on a minute—we need to talk!"

"Not now! Not today! I'm busy!"

Busy! she thought. Busy plaguin' somebody else. But he was tugging at his imprisoned wrist, plainly with half of his mind on getting free and the other half skittering away toward something up on the next rise. "Stand still! What ails you?" she demanded.

"*Ails* me?" He seemed astonished. "It's the Day! Ever'body's out and playin'! Be music and dancin' all night long! Don't you remember?"

Midsummer's Eve, he meant. Not the menacing Torskaal goings-on, but the Moorfolks' revels. She remembered the silvery *ting* of bells, the surging excitement—no work, all pranks and laughter, even younglings rollicking between Mound and moor, free of masters till dawn. Suddenly she remembered something else, and Tinkwa's words became a tool in her hand.

"*Ever'body's* out of the Mound," she echoed.

"In and out. Goin' and comin'."

"The Prince—him, too!"

She'd caught Tinkwa's full attention; he eyed her but did not speak.

She said softly, "Comes out Midsummer's Eve at sundown, the Prince does—doesn't he? Stays till near sunup. Same on May Day. Other times bides in the Mound."

"What's it to you where he's bidin'?" Tinkwa asked cautiously.

It might mean much to her before first light tomorrow, that was certain. Whenever the Prince left the Mound, the

205

door stayed open. When he returned, it shut fast, never mind who was caught inside. If she could wait through a nerve-racking day till sunset when the Prince fared forth, she and Tam would have all night to steal away the child.

"No matter," she told Tinkwa. He was already twisting in her grasp and peering over his shoulder. Like a grasshopper, his brain was. She took a bold risk and let him go. "If y'don't want me pipes, then be off with you!" she snapped at him.

He halted abruptly, halfway across the little hollow. "Your pipes? Eh, the chanter, belikes!"

"Nay, all of it! Drones, and bag and all! Real and true, I vow it!"

This time his attention focused sharply, his tilted eyes sparkled, speculated, then greened with suspicion as he peered at her bundle, at the ground beside her. "Where are they, then?"

She told him, adding, "Now, hark a minute!" as he exclaimed and started to turn away. "You'll have it all! Soon's you do what I want, I'll give you the chanter. Show that to Fergil and he'll give you the rest. He'll do it," she said to the doubt in Tinkwa's glance. "Pipes are nothin' to Fergil." She watched a new scheme sharpen the clever face and added, "Be nothin' to *you*, either, without the chanter." Deliberately, with his eyes following every move, she slipped the chanter into her shawl, tied the bundle around her waist, and clamped her elbow over it.

Tinkwa struggled visibly in her trap. But finally he shot her a sulky look and said, "So what must I do, then?"

Letting out the breath she'd been holding, she told him: lead her to the door, be her guide Inside, give warning before the Prince returned, get her back up the stair with a child.

He was full of objections. It might take too long; he'd miss the revels. He dassn't help sneak any child out— Pittittiskin'd have his hide.

"Guess I remembered you all wrong," Saaski taunted. "Used to be the boldest. 'Feared of nothin'! Dare anything, you would—or *said* you would."

He was silent. Then his wide, curled grin began to dawn; the lavender mischief gleamed in his eyes. "Eh, well . . . ," he said, and she'd won.

The rest was easy to agree on, its outcome hard to predict. The worst of it, to Saaski's mind, was the all-day wait. But wait they must; it was safer. Then in they'd go, the three of them—

"*Three* of us?" Tinkwa broke in.

"You and me—and me friend. Tam, the tinker's boy." She half turned, raised her voice. "Tam? Come on out."

Slowly Tam rose up from behind a thicket, plainly bursting with protest at her bargain, but minding his role to keep quiet. Tinkwa at once winked out. Transparent and wavery as smoke, he backed away, scowling and eyeing Tam sidewise. Saaski, tired of his caviling, demanded, "Now what? You've seen a boy afore, I reckon."

"Never reckoned havin' one go along of us. Into the Mound."

"Nor did I, but he's goin', 'less I can think how to stop 'im, which I haven't done yet. And *you're* makin' sure he gets out afore the Prince comes back, you hear me? Safe, and not a day older'n when he went in."

Tinkwa heard her in silence, his expression enigmatic, his glance slightly malicious.

"D'y'hear?" she insisted, sharp with anxiety. "Safe out before sunup! Swear it!"

But he would promise nothing, say nothing except, "Let nary a bite nor a sup pass his lips, then."

Tam waited with clamped jaw, eyes fixed on a place he apparently believed the voice to be coming from—though Tinkwa was a tether's length off to the left. "Leave off plaguin' and let 'im see you!" snapped Saaski, yanking at his arm.

"Why should I?" Tinkwa protested, but the shaking had ruined his wink-out, and he was there in plain sight, sulking.

"'Cause he best know you again." Once Tam had got a good look she loosed Tinkwa and stood away. "Go along with you now. We'll be here afore sundown—behind yonder thicket. Mind you're here, too."

He dived at once around the moorberry bushes and an instant later she saw him scampering—gray green and lizard swift—up a lichen-streaked rock face to join a dozen other half-glimpsed figures on the hillside, amid a burst of twittering in the old tongue.

Saaski watched with deep misgiving. "Might forget all about us."

"Hope he does!" Tam said resentfully. She turned

quickly, to find him scowling. "Eh, how could y'do it, Saaski? Let that little rogue have your pipes!"

"Only thing I've got to barter. Only thing he wants."

"But—how'll you get on without 'em? We might've found that door on our own—*you* might've . . ."

She shook her head. "Nay, Prince can hide it. He's full o' tricks. It'll be worth Da's pipes to trick *him* for a change."

"Wager he won't like it," Tam warned.

"*I'm* wagerin' he'll never know who did it. C'mon, stop your fretting," she added, with a glance toward the village. "Let's take the goats farther up."

Tam sighed but said no more, and they left the hollow, moving higher up the moor's shoulder, then higher yet, at Saaski's restless urging, till they were well out of sight of Torskaal land. Yet she kept glancing back, unable to feel safe from the pile of rowan wood at the boundary, which loomed in her mind like a pair of giant eyes fixed on her unblinkingly. She told herself that no villager would venture onto the moor Midsummer's Eve. But she continued to glance back.

Pulling up their hoods against a gust of wet wind, they took shelter under a gorse clump to let the rain pass. Tam broke a brooding silence. "One day, somehow or t'other, I'll get me hands on a set of bagpipes for you. See if I don't!" He gave a kick that sent some pebbles rattling downhill and added suddenly, "Here—I'll find a reed this day and whittle you a little pipe like mine! Then we can still play together, whenever we like!"

"Eh, that'll be fine," murmured Saaski, but she could not

imagine when or where they would do that, or picture anything at all, beyond sunup tomorrow. There seemed a lifetime of hours still to get through before it was even sundown tonight.

Then—it seemed almost too soon after all—it was late afternoon, and time to leave the safety of the high moor. They descended first to the tinker's hut, to tend and secure the animals for the night, since Tam had no faith that Bruman would do it. In fact, there was no sign of him.

"Gone a'ready!" Tam growled as he fetched water for the goats. "Couldn't wait to get down t'the Hillfire and all that free ale—sick 'n' sore as he is!"

They both glanced in the direction of the village, hidden below the slope of the moor. No sign of Bruman hobbling down toward it, either. Uneasily Saaski scanned the empty hillside, then, shivering at the thought of the rowan-wood tower waiting for the torch, she turned away hurriedly. Tam lingered for a last silent look at the worn hooded cart, the patient beasts—maybe, thought Saaski, wondering if he'd ever see them again.

"Don't go with me, Tam," she begged. "Best stay Outside, where you belong."

He merely said, "Nary a bite nor a sup. I'll mind that," and led the way uphill for their last climb of the day.

There was still a handsbreadth of golden sky between earth and sun when they reached the thorn-tree hollow and wriggled into the concealing thicket. A few wind-raveled clouds turned slowly scarlet; the light over the moor dimmed. To Saaski it seemed that time and sun both stopped; even the bird calls quieted. Then the sun's rim touched the edge of the earth.

First came a faint sound of bells, next of excited voices, growing rapidly louder and nearer—then a burst of chattering and music played helter-skelter on pipes and reeds and fiddles, the tunes all crisscrossing and near drowned out with laughter and thin shouting, and from behind a big boulder thrusting up through the grasses Moorfolk streamed until the hollow was filled with jostling, green-clad figures. In the midst of them came the Prince, jouncing on a straw-woven litter carried shoulder high by a dozen of his capering subjects. Saaski knew him at once—the beaky profile, the beard that waggled as he sang, the red jewel hanging around his neck and glowing like a drop of blood in the sun's low rays. His white hair thrust out like a thistle top from under his scarlet cap, and his long fingers beat the measure of whatever tune he was chanting. He glanced neither right nor left, and was swiftly borne past her hiding place toward the moor's crest, where he became one bobbing silhouette among many against the round gold sun.

"Now!" she gasped, and struggled free of twigs and thorns, peered about for Tinkwa, saw him running out from behind the big boulder and across the hollow after the others. She caught him before he got there, shook him to make him remember, turned to beckon to Tam and found him beside her. Clinging to Tinkwa she started back toward the boulder and saw the open door. By the instant of sundown, when below at the moor's edge the Hillfire leaped into a tower of flame from the villagers' torches, the three of them were halfway down the twisting stair.

211

Ten heartbeats after they disappeared from sight, Bruman, breathless, too, struggled up the opposite lip of the hollow, hobbled across it and around the boulder, blinked a dismayed instant from the narrow opening to his crutch, then flung away the crutch and squeezed in his turn through the door.

PART V

21

It was warm in the shadowy gloom of the stairwell, and smelled of earth and roots. Reckless of footing on the twisting, crooked steps, Saaski hurried after Tinkwa, one hand clutching his shoulder, the other Tam's coarse-woven sleeve. Half-glimpsed figures jostled past them, some crowding upward, a few rushing down, trailing snatches of chatter. Suddenly there came a cool draft wafting up, like a breath across snow, and a dim greenish glow flickered over the rough walls of the shaft ahead. The earthy odor gave way to a chill smell of stone, and the nearby gigglings and twitterings faded into an echoing confusion of many voices floating up from below. A few more turns of the stair and they were at the bottom, ducking out of a lopsided opening into a vast, green-lit space, and the confusion was all around them.

It was the Gathering—so much Saaski knew at once. And she had known it would be alive with Folk and their voices, no matter how many were Outside dancing on the moor or swarming up and down the stairs. What she had not expected was to be half stunned by the chaos of laughter and music and dashing about. She stopped where she was, engulfed by such an upsurge of old memory, old habit, that she could barely think, much less figure what to do next. Her hand went slack on Tinkwa's shoulder; he was gone at once. Her whole impulse was to dart away, too, join the nearest circle capering about a fiddler, snatch a handful of berries from the long tables, find old Flugenlul and steal his pipes . . .

"Lor'! Will you look at yon di'monds!" came Tam's hoarse whisper in her ear. "All over the ceilin', a million-million of 'em! An' rubies and suchlike on the walls, and all these grand lords and ladies, wearin' silks and furs and plumes in their hats—y'never told me it was like this here! It's finer than ever I saw in the King's Town, I vow 'tis!"

"What're y' sayin'?" gasped Saaski. She stared from Tam's marveling face to the rough rock walls of the Gathering, the faint crystalline glitter high on the dome overhead, the Folk in their shabby greenish tunics and scarlet caps. "It's the *glamourie!*" she exclaimed, giving his sleeve a sharp tug. "Don't heed it! Nothin's fine here, it's a trick—come along—"

"An' the feast laid out there!" Tam was saying, deaf to her warnings, already starting for the tables and pulling her along. "Never saw the like anywheres! Swans roasted with their feathers on, and whole great fishes—lookit the

216

cakes!—Lor', I'll wager it's that fairy mead in the flagons yonder . . ."

Saaski gave his arm a yank with her whole strength behind it, and he half fell toward her, protesting as he caught his balance. "Come away, I said!" she shrieked at him. "There's no swans and fishes there, it's dock an' sorrel boiled with turnips or some such—an' moorberries an' bog water . . . Come *away*, Tam!"

"But there's oranges! I'll just have a taste . . ."

"Ye'll taste nothin', y'*mustn't!* Not a bite nor a sup—don't y'remember?" Saaski pled with him—and at last he looked at her and seemed to recollect himself.

"Aye, I mind now—nary a bite nor a sup. Here, let's get out'n this place—away from them tables!"

"But I dunno where to go . . ." The frantic need to cope with Tam had at least jarred her momentarily out of her own dreaming, loosed the pull of the old life. She must stay free of it until she'd found the child. *Don't think how it used to be,* she told herself sternly. *Not yet. Don't think of nothin' but Mumma's child.*

"Where's that Tinkwa?" Tam demanded.

"Got away from me," she confessed. "Up on the moor by now, for all I know. He'll come back afore the Prince does—he wants me pipes! Don't rightly need 'im till then, 'cause I mind now where the Nursery is—if I can work out how to get there."

She started for the far end of the Gathering, threading her way among the cookfires and the milling Folk, still with a firm grip on Tam's sleeve. He lagged often, exclaiming over some wonder only he could see, or begging her to stop

217

a moment to hear a fiddler's tune. She merely insisted, "I dassn't! I dassn't!" and tugged him on. It was hard enough to keep her mind on what she was doing; distractions clutched at her from every direction. A familiar lithe figure with floating hair darted past, stopped abruptly, and turned to stare at her; another slipped up beside her to tweak her apron ties, poke at her bundle; a third and fourth stood whispering together, watching her with tilted lavender eyes, and one of them said, "Moql?"

Then the other crowed with laughter and seized her hand, ripping her away from Tam and into a wildly whirling dance that left her giggling and excited, with no desire to do anything but join the next circle that swept her up— and the next, and the next.

Time slowed and raced bewilderingly; she lost all sense of it until she spun out of the dance and sagged breathless against an earthen doorway, groping after some urgent purpose that eluded her. Frowning about, she found herself on a familiar—yet oddly unfamiliar—threshold. This low, rough arch like the entrance to an animal's den—could this be the door to Schooling House? Surely that was larger, more welcoming . . .

Welcoming? *Help me!* Her own voice echoed chillingly in her memory. There'd been no welcome the last time she had gone through that door. And no help, either.

This time someone was helping her—she knew someone was—though not where he was . . . But why was it she needed help?

It came back in a rush. Tam. *Tam.* And the child.

She looked around wildly, caught a glimpse of Tam's dark hair and gangling figure amongst a circle of dancers halfway across the great cave. He was laughing, lurching as they tugged him this way and that in the complex patterns of the dance. She pushed her way toward him, fending off reaching hands, trying not to hear or see or think until she got a firm grasp on his arm. At last she had it, and pulled and shrieked at him until he broke out of the melee and stumbled after her, to the nearest rocky wall.

"I lost you!" he gasped, leaning against the rugged surface.

"We lost each other! And we mustn't, d'y'hear? We dassn't! I—I'm still—" She broke off. *I'm still half Folk,* was what she was realizing, with something like fright. *Neither one thing nor yet quite t'other.* The Folk half wanted only to dance and tease and cared for nothing but the Paths and the Band. The other half wanted to pay the Prince out, give Mumma back her child. And which half would win? The Folk half could barely remember the mission. "Lost meself, too, for a while," she told Tam shakily. "Keep tight holt o' me! Don't let me loose."

His hand closed on hers. "I won't. I won't. Eh . . . it was jolly, though, that dance!"

"Don't think of it. Come along!"

Again she headed for a door she knew was somewhere on the opposite side of the Gathering from the winding stair. This time she stayed close to the uneven stony wall, away from the comings and goings and whirlings in the center. Tam ducked repeatedly to avoid the jutting overhang of rock that easily cleared Folk heads; even Saaski had to crouch at times, but she kept a sharp eye scanning the shadows nearest the wall, and was finally rewarded with a glimpse of smooth-worn wood.

"There!" she exclaimed. Swiftly she dodged into a narrow cleft blocked by a wooden door. Tam, bent almost double, stumbled after her. A push on the wear-darkened edge of the door's panel and it turned on its pivot to open a slit at each side.

"Lor! I can't get through there!" Tam muttered, but he squeezed through after her somehow, and the way opened slightly, zigzagging upward.

The door creaked closed behind them as they rounded an angle of rock and stepped into a corridor patterned with shadows and pierced at intervals with glimmering openings.

At once it was easier to think, to keep her mind clear of confusion, of waves of forgetful excitement. After a moment to get her bearings, Saaski crossed to peer cautiously through the first doorway into an arched, cavelike room. It was lighted dimly but steadily by glowworms clinging to the rocky wall and coldfire torches stuck here and there into the sandy floor. A whiff of cool, earth-scented air came out to meet them, along with a sound of tiny stirrings and snufflings, an occasional muffled peep, that put her in mind of a nest of hatching chicks.

"It's the Nursery," she whispered, pointing to the row of little roundish cribs around its edge.

She tiptoed in, alert for the old Moorwomen who should be here, guarding the little ones—oftentimes with the aid of servants enticed or captured from Outside. At first she saw no one; then across the room she spied a lone aged figure curled up on a pile of bracken, asleep like her charges. Beyond, a dimly glowing archway led into some farther chamber, and a Folk-shaped shadow flitted across it. There was no sign of the child.

"Golden cradles they have!" breathed Tam, who was peeking wide-eyed into the nearest of the tiny beds. "Sleepin' on eiderdown like little lords!"

It was only thistledown, and his golden cradles were nothing but rough grass baskets lined with leaves. He was off on his marveling again, and it was worrisome—suppose they both forgot what they had come for? But Saaski wasted no time arguing. Instead, she peered around for a pot of the ointment she knew must be here in the Nursery somewhere, for it was used daily on the babies. One touch of it on his eyelids and he would see what the Folk saw, not the *glamourie* conjured up to blind and bedazzle Outsiders.

She spied a squat stone jar on a shelf, darted to it and had just dipped a finger in when something blotted out the light from the archway across the room and one of the ancient caretakers came hobbling toward them scolding shrilly in the old tongue.

Saaski retreated hastily, twittering apologies. "Only me, Nursie! Meant no harm—we're off now, gone . . ." She backed out into the corridor, turning to push Tam ahead of her into the shadows clustered next to the wall.

"Here! Did y'see that?" Tam was exclaiming, dropping his voice to a whisper as Saaski shushed him, but twisting to look over his shoulder. "Wearin' a crown, she was! They got *queens* to look after'em, the little 'uns! What was she sayin' to you?"

"Tellin' us to clear off! Hsst! Just stand here quiet . . ." They were huddled behind a jutting chunk of rock. Saaski waited until she heard the muttering that told her the old nurse had hobbled back into her earthen realm, then turned swiftly to dab her finger's worth of ointment over Tam's nearest eyelid. She reached toward the other but before she could touch it he dodged, protesting, and the last of the ointment was lost in his hair.

"Eh, what've y' done!" she gasped, peering down at her finger, which was wiped clean.

"What were *you* doin, pokin' your finger in me eye?" he asked in bewilderment.

"Only tryin'—to make things easier." She drew a quivering long breath, hoping she had not made them harder than ever. From now on Tam would see truth with one eye, but diamonds and golden cradles with the other. It seemed no use stopping to explain. "Come on, that next room yonder might be Spinning House . . ."

But the next faintly glowing breach in the wall opened into the byre for the red-horned cattle; so much was plain to their noses if not to their eyes; the one torch lit only an empty cavern. The cattle, too, were out on the moor tonight. Saaski pulled Tam on to the final doorway. One swift glance into a wide, low room showed her idle looms, a work-scarred table littered with spindles, piles of tattered wool-gleanings and the wads of cobwebs she had always known would be there. Shelves held earth-green homespun and a bolt or two of paler cloth that shimmered with cob-web iridescence and stirred gently, as if too bubble-light to settle down. It was Spinning House—tonight silent and deserted in the vaguely pulsing glow lights.

Cautiously she stepped in. The doorway was wide, but low enough to make Tam duck, and as he straightened she waited nervously for the first test of his mismatched eyes. For a moment he merely blinked as he glanced around him, muttered, "Lor!" then frowned and rubbed his right eye—it was the one she had touched with the ointment.

"What d'y see?" Saaski whispered.

"Piles 'o gold stuff—are they *fleeces*? And silks an'. . . Here! It's that spinning room, a'nt it? Yonder's looms and suchlike, all silver and jewels—" He rubbed his eye again. "Whatja do to me eye, then? Feels half-blinded!"

"Cover the other one," Saaski told him.

He did so, and the sudden dismay on his face told her all she needed to know. With both eyes open, plainly the *glam-ourie* outbedazzled the shabby reality. But he was seeing truth now. Before she could urge him to keep the lying eye covered, he abruptly used both hands to seize her shoulders and draw her back into the shadows. She turned and at once forgot everything else.

From the inner doorway a small figure was crossing the room toward the cluttered table—a little girl with dark, loose-hanging hair, nearly Saaski's height, though she was chubbier and younger. Despite her greenish Folk garments, she was not Folk; she had neither the long hands and feet nor the alert, darting glance. She was a human child.

223

But there was nothing childlike about her dull, listless expression, her drifting progress across the room. *Not the one*, Saaski told herself quickly. *Mistake*.

Then the child's head turned, and the greenish torchlight fell full on her face. It was a round, dark-browed face, set with sky-blue eyes that made Saaski catch her breath, for they were Anwara's own.

There could be no mistake. This was Mumma's child.

22

Sasski stepped forward into the light, drawing Tam with her, and the child halted. The blue eyes glanced, unsurprised, at Saaski, but widened at sight of Tam. She shrank back a little and stood staring at him.

"Don't be afeard. Nobody's gonna hurt you," Saaski assured her. She got nothing but a slow, uncomprehending look in reply.

"Is she deef?" Tam muttered.

To Saaski it seemed more as if she were sleepwalking—or entranced. *And that might be,* she thought with a little thrill of fear. She moved cautiously to the table, reached across it and touched the child's arm. "Can y'understand what I'm sayin'?" she demanded. Then on a sudden thought she repeated the question in the old tongue.

After a moment the child said softly, "I can."

"She talks Folkish," Saaski told Tam in relief. "Reckon she's never heard anything else." In the old tongue, she asked the child her name.

"Lekka," was the answer.

It was not even a real name—merely the word for *stolen*. The indifference of it—the Folkishness—made Saaski angry. "Aye, you *were* stolen. It's so. You don't belong here. You're human—like him! See his eyes? Here, look close! Yours're blue, like that. Your hair's dark like his. You've got a mumma and da'—Outside. We'll take you back to 'em."

For a moment she thought she had got through the fog of enchantment to the brain within; a puzzled frown passed across the child's placid forehead, something stirred in her eyes. Then it was gone; her face was again smooth and passive. "I'm not to go through the Turning Door. I'm to finish these fleeces," she said. She sat down at the table by a wad of gleanings and began picking the thorny twigs and leaf bits out of it. Her fingertips were already rough and sore-looking from such work.

"Eh, you're nothin' but a slavey!" Saaski said indignantly. "You don't want to stay here, won't y' come with us?" She reached for the reddened little hand, but the child evaded her.

"What's goin' on?" Tam demanded.

"Can't get through to 'er! Tried explainin', tried coaxin', but they've got 'er spellbound or some such, she just—"

"Try plain *tellin'* 'er," Tam said. "She'll likely mind you—y'look like Folk." He glanced over his shoulder, into the corridor, rubbing uneasily at his eye. "We can't bide here! Night's passin'—and we're a long ways from out!"

He was right. Here there was no moon, no changing sky to tell them how far the night had advanced while they were dancing with the revelers, locating the Turning Door—or how soon the Prince would tire of the moor and come back to the Mound, sealing the stairway to all but Folk. Heartened because Tam sounded again like Tam, not the *glamourie*-befuddled stranger the Mound had made of him—and hoping his one anointed eye would keep him so—Saaski turned to the child. This time she simply grasped the chubby hand, removed the twiggy fleece from it, and gave it a firm pull. "Come, Lekka! You're to go with us," she commanded.

Without protest the child arose, came obediently around the table, and followed her out of the room, back along the shadowy corridor past the dimlit Nursery, where a stooped silhouette told Saaski that old Nursie was still on guard. A few steps farther brought them safe onto the last steep slope to the pivoting door.

Here Lekka ceased to be docile. Her hand jerked out of Saaski's; she backed away.

"Here! What're y' up to? Come along!" Saaski whispered, clutching at her in the gloom.

"I'm not to go through the Turning Door," the child said clearly.

"Hssst! Be quiet!" Saaski made a frantic grab and tried to tug her forward. Lekka planted her feet.

"I'm not to—," the clear voice began.

It was muffled by Tam's big hand. He said nothing, merely picked the child up bodily, pushed her face into the folds of smocking at his shoulder, and jerked his head toward the door. Saaski's swift push turned it on its pivot and he struggled through, Lekka prisoned in his arms.

"Didn't I say ye'd need me to carry 'er?" he was panting to Saaski as she ran ahead along the final narrow cleft into the Gathering.

She never answered. The burst of voices and greenish light and rushing motion engulfed her again, all but swept her away. She reached dizzily for the rocky wall beside her, grasped a handful of Tam's ragged cloak, and clung to it. "Best hang on to me," she gasped.

"I can't hang on to the two of ye!" he protested. However, he swung Lekka to the sandy floor, keeping a wary eye on her while he reached backward to Saaski. Then his voice softened with surprise. "Eh, look at that, will ye!"

Saaski tore her attention from a circle dance forming nearby and with an effort focused it on Lekka. The child was blinking up into Tam's face with bright, interested eyes, and tentatively smiling. The change was astonishing.

"She's come out of it! Likely because of passin' through that door." Saaski's gaze lingered on the now vivid little face, and a strange wistfulness drifted over her, as though some inner door in herself had briefly opened on an unknown landscape of feelings. *Eh, Mumma, I warrant you'll like this gift*, she thought.

"What now?" Tam demanded, pulling her back to herself.

"First we hide this child," she told him.

228

"Where? In me pocket?" Tam's grin appeared, and Lekka peered up at him and grinned back.

"She likes you. That'll help," Saaski said. "'Cause I think you best take 'er on your back—I'll put your cloak over the both of you, and the hood over her head."

Swiftly, in the old tongue, she told Lekka what they were doing, and Tam hoisted the child up, wrapping his arms firmly about her chubby legs. "Next?" he said.

Next she had to find Tinkwa. Only Folk could get Tam up those stairs and out of the Mound unchanged, unharmed. No use searching the ever-shifting groups of dancers for one particular capering figure. If Tinkwa was here, he could elude her forever; if he had fled out onto the moor, forgetting—*eh, well, then*, she thought, *the rascal'll never get me pipes*.

Nothing to do but make for the stairway entrance and hope he'd be there, waiting. She could see it, directly across the expanse of the Gathering—a lopsided archway in the rocky wall. Perhaps it could all be over and done with in one bold moment.

"Come!" she cried, with an imperative yank on Tam's hand, and plunged into the shifting throng, heading straight for the stair.

It was like plunging into a whirlwind, with a bog underfoot. Greenish forms bumped and jostled her from all sides, laughter mocked her; a mudlike dragging on her feet transformed her dash into a dream struggle in which she could scarcely see or move at all. She came to herself flattened breathless against the same wall she had left, feeling as if

she had been flung against it. Tam, with Lekka still clinging on his back, was standing anxiously in front of her,
breathless too. The child looked wide-eyed and startled.

It had been easy enough to go deeper and deeper into the
Mound. But every step in the other direction was impeded,
as if the Mound itself were taunting them. *You've managed
to get in, have you? Let's see you get out.*

Angry tears sprang to Saaski's eyes. *But it's me! Moql!* part
of her was protesting though she knew well that she was not
Moql, would never be Moql again. *Y'don't rule me now,* she
told the Mound defiantly. *I'll get us all out, you watch!*

Tam gave a hitch to his passenger, scowling uneasily
about him. "That stair keeps movin'! Here—then yonder!
How'll we ever get to it?"

"You're seein' things again!" sighed Saaski, struggling to
get her wits together. To Lekka, she said in the old tongue,
"Put your hand over his left eye. Keep it there."

The child hesitated, but obeyed. Tam's face went blank
and surprised, then an expression of chagrin settled over it
as his gaze fixed on the entrance—unmoved from where it
had been all along. But he only muttered, "Eh, this is a rare,
contrarious place!"

"It is," said Saaski grimly. "So now we'll try walkin' back-
wards."

She turned herself about, and Tam, blinking and grumbling a bit under Lekka's persistent hand, turned, too. At
once they began to make progress. So it was *some* use to be
half Folk, and no stranger to Folk cunning. Now, if Tinkwa
were there, waiting . . .

They were halfway to the rough archway when a long-fingered hand reached suddenly out of nowhere to tug at her arm, pulling her off balance and back toward the wall she was fighting to escape. "Leave go!" she exclaimed, and turned to find Tinkwa beside her, panting and breathless.

"C'mon, c'mon! Prince is comin' in, be quick!"

"But that's the wrong—" She looked wildly over her shoulder toward the stairway entrance. "Where're you takin' us?"

"Don't argufy! C'mon!"

He, too, flung a swift glance toward the stair, and gave her wrist a yank of surprising strength. She could do nothing but stumble after him.

"Should I clout 'im a good 'un?" puffed Tam ferociously, close by her ear.

"Nay—leave 'im be! Likely knows what he's doin'." She could only hope she was right—and that he hadn't left it far too late. She could hear a faint chiming of bells echoing from the stairwell, the voice of a horn, and a stir of fresh excitement in the Gathering. Plainly, the Prince was all but on the stairs.

"In here!" ordered Tinkwa, shoving her ahead of him into the narrow cleft they had so recently left. "Go on, in with ye! You, too!" he snapped at Tam. "Or stay behind if y'like!"

But Saaski, confronted again by the Turning Door, set her heels and faced him. "We've just come from here, you rascal! What kind of rare trick are you playin'?"

"No trick, I vow it! Jus' through that door, and sneak past the babies—"

"Easy to say! That Nursie'll cotch us sure this time—and we can't hide for long in Spinning House!"

"No need to!" Tinkwa was all but jumping up and down with anxiety. "Get on with it, will ye? Through the door!"

"But there's no way out!"

"There is! D'ye think they take the red-horns up those stairs?"

She stared at him an instant, then gasped, "Tam! Come!" and squeezed through the Turning Door, Tinkwa after her. But Tam did not follow. Holding the door on its pivot and peering back through the slit she saw him rock-still in the narrow passage, staring back through the cleft into the Gathering. "Tam! *Tam!*" she insisted—then saw that he was holding Lekka's hand away from his lying eye.

She darted back down to him. *"You must come!"* she all but shrieked at him, seizing his arm and shaking it with all her strength.

Then, at last, he turned, clapped Lekka's hand over his eye again, and followed her.

Stumbling with relief, she led the way through the Turning Door and along the shadowy corridor, Tinkwa now harrying them from behind and all but snapping at their heels, past the Nursery and into the byre—still redolent of the red-horns, but still empty.

"Behind the last stall—quick!" Tinkwa hissed at them.

They plunged through a dark opening into a rocky tunnel that sloped upward and showed, far ahead, an irregular patch of light. Saaski ran eagerly, wildly, elated as always to be heading for the moor. When they burst out at last into the mild, heather-scented air of a summer daybreak she felt such joy that she would have kept on running straight ahead had Tinkwa not yanked her behind the same big boulder that hid the stair. Tam dropped down beside them, panting, easing Lekka to the ground and flinging his cloak over her. Through a screen of brush Saaski saw the hillside suddenly swarm with capering figures. Then the piping and the fiddles and the bells filled her ears as the Prince and his troupe came dancing across her thorny peephole, blotting out the last stars in the paling sky. They passed within arm's length to descend into the Mound.

The voices and music grew rapidly fainter, faded, were abruptly silenced as by the closing of a door. After a moment a drowsy bird cheeped.

23

Tinkwa was the first to recover, straightening from his crouch to grin and dart a lavender glance at Saaski. "Near cotched us," he remarked.

"Too near, thanks to you!" Her heart was thumping wildly, whether from fright or relief or sudden wretchedness at that abrupt silence she scarcely knew.

She stood up, hesitated, then slipped around to the other side of the boulder and gazed bleakly but without surprise at an undisturbed stretch of ordinary rocks and heather, just visible in the predawn light. Of the door into the Mound she could see nothing—and likely never would again.

She was turning away when she saw the crutch. A stifled exclamation, a moment's incredulous staring, and she went over to pick it up. Another instant she stood with it in her hands, then moved back around the boulder. "Tam . . . ?" she said.

He was confronting Tinkwa—the Folk could never again hide from his anointed right eye—but he turned when she spoke, looked at the crutch she was holding out to him, and nodded. "He's back inside there—in the Mound."

"You *saw* 'im?"

"When we were leavin'."

Saaski drew in her breath. No puzzle now, why he had stood there rock-still in the passageway, deaf to her urgings.

"Hoaxed us for certain-sure, didn't 'e? Reckon he aimed to all along," Tam said thoughtfully.

Saaski hesitated, then asked, "See him eat anything?"

"Eatin' and drinkin' with both hands, he was— a-purpose." Tam turned again to Tinkwa. "Here!—how long afore he's free?"

"Prince'll throw 'im out when he's a mind to," Tinkwa evaded. He edged away, tugging at Saaski. "The chanter! Gi'me the chanter!"

Tam seized his arm and held him. "Tell me *when*."

"I dunno! Time runs different . . . Twelvemonth an' a day, mebbe. Or seven year. Or five-an'-fifty." He shrugged, pulled free. "Or mebbe two hun'ert," he added.

"*Two hun'ert year?*" Tam whispered.

Tinkwa was dancing with impatience. "The chanter! Give it to me! Y'vowed I'd have it!"

"Aye, y'will, y'will!" Saaski loosed the shawl from around

her waist, worked at the stubborn knots, then—quickly, before she let herself think about it—drew out the chanter and gave it to him. He snatched it with a crow of triumph, and was gone, leaping and capering down the hillside toward Moor Water and Fergil's hut, already piping one of the wild Folkish tunes.

She turned her back on him. Tam had not moved, but stood staring at nothing—or maybe into the void of two hundred years.

"Likely Bruman got what he wanted," she ventured.

"Aye. Raised 'is glass to me and laughed like I haven't seen 'im laugh since I dunno when." Tam smiled crookedly himself. "I took a look with me lyin' eye—to see what he was seein'. Eh . . . it was rare and wondrous, right enough . . ." He took a long breath. "Too late to mend, anywise. But s'pos'n that Prince throws 'im out afore he's ready?"

"You might could come back in a twelvemonth an' a day—just to see."

"We will. And mebbe in seven year." Tam roused himself, adding firmly, "But now we're leavin'—the both of us! No more'n an hour to sunup—by then you best be gone."

"There's still the child."

Tam seemed suddenly to realize the plan was not finished. He swung around to peer toward Lekka, still huddled under his cloak. "Ye'll never take 'er clean into t'village!" he said in alarm. "Y'dassn't show yourself!"

"Nay, I'll take her to Gran'mum—Old Bess," Saaski amended. "Easy to reach her cottage and nobody the wiser. Done it lots o' times."

"Then let's be at it," Tam said. He bent to lift the cloak off Lekka, gave a startled exclamation and froze, one edge held wide. Even before she moved to look, Saaski guessed what she would see: a child either older or younger than the one they had stolen out of the Mound.

She was younger, much younger—soundly sleeping, one hand curled beside a chubby cheek, a thumb in her mouth, fine dark ringlets clustered over a still babyish head. The green Folkish garments were now absurdly oversized. She looked barely of an age to toddle—let alone, Saaski thought suddenly, able to make the long, rough walk down to Torskaal, and that before sunup.

"I'll have t'carry her down," she said, and wondered if she could. The child was plump and sturdily built, for all her babyishness.

"Nay, we'll take 'er in the cart," Tam said. "It's mine now, I reckon—for a twelvemonth. Mebbe forever. Pony and goats and old Warrior, too. Come on, Lekka—" He woke the child gently, let her blink up at him a moment, and set her on her feet. Saaski moved closer, stretched out a hand. But at sight of her Lekka shrank away and clung to Tam.

Thinks I'm Folk. Saaski withdrew the hand. After a moment she managed a shrug. "Can't say I blame her for shyin' off. She trusts you, anywise."

Tam picked the child up, grinned briefly. "Little she knows!" he said. "If I'd had my way she'd still be pluckin' thorns and such out'n gleanings, 'cause we'd never've gone in that Mound."

He started downhill, toward Bruman's deserted hut, the

animals and cart. Before she turned to follow, Saaski glanced once more around the hollow with the thorn trees, then out over the moor in the direction Tinkwa had gone. He would go back into the Mound when he had her pipes in his hands, and be at home. But she no longer belonged there. In truth she did not even belong to the moor in the way she once had, when she was Moql—the way Tinkwa and the others did. Part and parcel of it, the Folk were, same as the heather and the bogs. As for the King's Town and the fairs and the land far south by the Long Sea, where she supposed they were going—she could not imagine she would ever belong there, either.

But she was sure she belonged with Tam.

Now she thought of it, he belonged nowhere, either—and seemed to like it just that way.

By dawn the old hooded cart was skreaking and rattling down the hillroad at the far end of the village in the pink-and-golden light, the goats ambling alongside and Warrior trotting behind. Tam pulled up in a thicket's shelter, tied the pony to a branch, and lifted Lekka down. A few swift strides and he was knocking softly at Old Bess's door.

It opened almost at once. With a muffled exclamation the old woman stepped out, stood an instant, then took the child into her arms. Little was said; little needed saying. And then Tam was slapping the reins over the pony's rump, and the cart began its swaying, creaking journey back up the steep track over the moor in the direction of the distant town.

Old Bess waited, standing tall and still on her doorstep, holding her grandchild. She was rewarded by a glimpse of a long-fingered hand, thrust between the old leather curtains at the cart's rear, waving. Old Bess waved back until the cart crested the hill and she could no longer look into the rising sun.

24

As the years passed over Torskaal, the villagers almost forgot the changeling who had once lived there, pretending to be a child. Old Bess did not, but she kept her thoughts and memories to herself. Her grandchild Leoran grew and bloomed, and spun the smoothest thread and wove the tightest cloth of any child along the street. She was prettier than most, too. Yanno looked at her and marveled at her delicacy and that he had had any part in it. Sometimes, as he worked at his skeps, with the scent of rosemary heavy on the summer air, he wished she were not so timid around the bees, and allowed his mind to wander back to other days. But he could not help being glad she feared the moor, and would never go next or nigh it.

As for Anwara, her voice had softened and her bony

shoulders grew plump and her waistline plumper yet, and her eyes were proud as she watched her daughter grow.

Only sometimes, on a still evening, or at midday when she rested from her weeding in the highfield, she fancied she heard the high, shrill wail of a piper, playing the strange, wild tunes she remembered. Once she even climbed past the edge of Torskaal land and onto the moor, half fearing, half expecting to see a familiar aproned figure with a pale bush of hair playing on Yanno's da's pipes. Instead she glimpsed a very small green-clad piper perched atop a rock—and next minute saw nothing at all.

And there was a time she fancied she heard the sound of two shepherd's pipes in unison, playing, most beautifully, the same strange tunes.

But she was never sure about that.